Born in the Isle of Man in the '60s (1960s and not 1860s) Gaz is a family man who loves spending time with his family and walking his dogs on the beautiful beaches around the island. He is also passionate about his football and never lets that dampen his light-hearted mood.

This book is dedicated to all the fun loving people across the world that don't take life too seriously, and are very, very easily amused.

Gaz Quaggan

BUT NOT BIG TO DINOSAURS

THE INCOMPLETE WORKS OF PANTSRANTIANS

AUSTIN MACAULEY
PUBLISHERS LTD.

A CIP catalogue record for this title is available from the British Library.

ISBN 9781786125903 (Paperback)
ISBN 9781786125910 (Hardback)
ISBN 9781786125927 (E-Book)
www.austinmacauley.com

First Published (2016)
Austin Macauley Publishers Ltd.
25 Canada Square
Canary Wharf
London
E14 5LQ

Printed in the UK

Contents

Calm Indignations on Precipitous Vibrations!

So ... do oranges have testicles?

Now you might be thinking that I've just asked a totally ridiculous and frankly weird question, but no ... I haven't. Now I ask because surely they can't have as if they did, then they'd no longer work would they? I mean – how could they after having been systematically <<love that infrequently used word, word – Alert>> squashed all of their 'pre' and 'post' orange tree lives. Now you might be pondering <<not a word for the study of small bodies of water, word – Alert>> there a bit (or a lot) as to what the blooming heck are an orange's life stages ... and indeed what's an adult orange versus ... err ... a juvenile or infant one?

Well – luckily fir you, and before we delivevintinthusceeeks (I actually typed 'delve into this week's' there but alas ... big fingers win yet again) rant, I can advise that oranges and their sex organs aren't necessarily gonna be the theme of this week's nonsense. That said, however, I am actually gonna talk about oranges for just a wee (but not pee) while and explain about their adulthood versus childhood stages and their apparent lack of working testicles ... as I know you're just itching to know more. Oh – but before I do, can I just very quickly go back and correct a typo that I've just noticed … as I clumsily typed the word 'fir' back there when of course I actually meant 'for'. Please just ignore this oversight – as it's typed now … and anyhow 'fir' is an animal's sorta winter clothes and thus totally different from the word 'for' which is of course just a word meaning 'intended to be given to' … or indeed a 'misspelt word for a number greater than three and one less than five'!

Now please forgive me one final diversion (it won't be), but I just really have to go back to that big mistyped word nonsense 'delivevintinthusceeeks' which of course had to have one of those really annoying red-lines underneath it … meaning it was either a) an incorrect spelling or b) not in fact a real word. So, okay – and perhaps that's fairly acceptable (if not tedious) of you 'Mr Smarty-Pants Spell Check' to correct my literary misdemeanours <<fairly lengthy word and one that makes you look clever, word – Alert>>. But oh no, you wouldn't let it lie there would you. I mean … so what happens when I confusedly but obediently click onto the red underlined word to get the correct spelling? Fuck-bloody-fuck-all … that's what. Well okay – it offered me up the totally freaking pointless and useless – 'No Replacements' – but what the hell's the use of that? I mean … isn't my iPad supposed to be like the most intelligent thing in the world and even cleverer than that weird synthesizer speaking scientific has-been in the wheelchair … eh? Oh freaking no … it's not. In fact – it's friggin thicker than me … and I'm so thick I can get lost in an empty room of a doll's house!

And so … swiftly back to oranges, which although aren't (maybe) the main topic of this week's diatribe <<not a word meaning to colour-stain an indigenous group of people, word – Alert>> it is a subject that's alas gonna use up a fair bit of my 'finger ink'. Oh – and incidentally … if you're interested (which I'll wager you're not) I'm not one of these 'nimble-fingered' clever clogs sorts who can speedily and effortlessly (and annoyingly if I'm honest) type using both their thumbs. Oh no … I'm actually a mono-digit-typing buffoon who is unable to multi task and as such I excruciatingly churn out all this bollox using only my right index finger! So … err, oh … I hope you don't mind hanging on one more minute before I rant about oranges or indeed this week's subject matter (whatever that is), it's just that I now feel the irresistible urge to quickly revert back to the phrase 'clever-clogs'. They're not. Nope … they're just wooden shoes. In fact, there's absolutely nothing remotely 'intellectual' about them as they're just 'made of trees' impractical and uncomfortable footwear from Holland. Now Holland is also known as the Netherlands … which if I'm totally honest is a bit of a worry 'cos 'Nether' means 'Never' … so in reality – the place shouldn't exist! But it does of course.

Now whilst I think the Dutch are 'nice' people – you've gotta admit that they know absolutely bugger all about cobbling – aka the making of shoes. I mean how could they, as there's absolutely no need to wear shoes in Holland as its landscape is made up entirely of just flat fields of tulips. Now please don't get me wrong … I'm not actually criticizing the people from Holland … but you've gotta admit that they're a bit strange. I mean although they love dykes (don't all men), they all live in windmills, ride bicycles and eat garlic … oh hang about though – that's the French who like the garlic (or likes zee garlics) … as they would say in 'Froggish' … the national language of France. But they are just like the French them Dutch fools (typed 'folks' there – but let's

17

run with it anyway) as they even speak the same ridiculous language … you know – Double Dutch!

Oh – okay … so the people from the Netherlands (which doesn't exist) actually speak a repetitive (must be – hence the name) 'Double Dutch' dialect, and the Frogs (official collective name for nationals of France) speak 'Froggish', but in reality they're both the same. Well, they are in my opinion – as they're both 'all Greek to me' … and to be totally honest – English is the language they should really both use as surely it's the only one with any 'international' credibility. Now please don't fret – as when I mentioned 'my opinion' back there – I wasn't being all presumptuous <<don't have the foggiest idea what that word means, word – Alert>> as I fully accept that opinions are like 'assholes' … everyone has one. Now please – it's important to remember here that I'm not biased <<not a word for a person with two bottoms, word – Alert>> towards the English language as I'm not even British – let alone from England. But surely you've gotta admit that other languages (in comparison … or not) are just a bit rubbishy and don't really stack up or pass the 'smell test' of reality.

I mean how successful would the Beatles have been singing – 'Tout ce que vous avez besoin est amour, l'amour, l'amour est tout ce que vous avez besoin' … instead of the universally understood English love related version. Eh? Not freaking very … is the answer, as the French version (and I've nothing at all against the Froggies – as I love garlic, string onion necklaces, silly black hats and … err … the lower limbs of edible green amphibians) is about 1,000 words long. Oh and what about America's – 'The White House' … in Dutch it's 'Het Witte Huis' – which just doesn't quite 'float the boat' of importance and power does it! Eh? Anyhow,

I've really, really digressed this time – and further off course than an excitable Absinthe fuelled nomad astride a camel on heat … so finally, it's back to oranges and testicles. So, what the friggin' heck am I going on about this week?

Well … do oranges have testicles, you know – balls or bollox? Now surely they can't have as due the restrictive packaging they have to endure all their lives (from baby pips to juvenile fruit to adult fresh juice) they'd be totally freaking destroyed – or (groan-alert) bolloxed! So … what blooming packaging I hear you ask? Well – the one which they have to wear and are all wrapped throughout their complete lives. Now before you call the loony-bin ambulance to come and collect me … hear us out … as the evidence is totally compelling (maybe). Okay … so as a pip or seed – they're squished inside a sorta tiny hard shell-like thing. Now that's gotta be uncomfortable … and (groan – alert) ex-seed-ingly unbearable.

Then, as they're hanging around on trees, the poor juvenile oranges are all packed up inside a very tight and impossibly restrictive leathery-orangey skin. Those poor teenage* oranges' gonads (you might wanna google that … or not) must be absolutely squeezed beyond bloody belief being constricted tightly inside their airtight orange-peel 'gimp' suits. Now you might be thinking here, if your brain hasn't already shut down in despair (it will), maybe their testicles are not actually on the inside. Well no – as that'd be nonsense. I mean have you ever seen an orange with bollox on the outside? No, of course you haven't … and if you have, then you need to either drink less of that aforementioned <<long word meaning something said earlier, word – Alert>> Absinthe or cut down on the magic mushrooms. So, if oranges do have testicles (which of course the men ones must – or else how would they breed with lady oranges and make baby oranges) then they must be an internal organ, you know, on the inside! Oh before I go on (and on) I must just go back to that little asterisk '*' thingy I typed back there. Now this wasn't actually a typo but deliberate as a kinda 'clarification reference' ... you know, like you see on important clever documents and stuff. So I thought that I'd better just clarify (in case you're wondering – which you won't be) how oranges age. Well, there's an extremely complex and scientific calculation formula behind this ... but for ease and simplicity let's just say 1 x human year = 50 x orange ones.

And of course it doesn't get any freaking better for oranges when they finally achieve adulthood or attain their juice life-cycle stage. I mean even if their ingrown fruity 'danglers' had survived their extreme tightly-packed childhood ... they're then squashed to smithereens <<great word that sounds like it means, word – Alert>> as they're liquidized to make freshly squeezed orange juice. Now as if that wasn't bad enough for the poor oranges' testicles ... they're then injected (and at very high pressure) into silly rectangular cartons. And if, by some completely unimaginable miracle, their bollox had survived all of this ... they're then once again compacted beyond belief by the orange-juice cartons being smothered by a covering of $(C_2H_4)nH_2$ ... or polythene to you and I. And oh boy, this polythene skin is the tightest fitting thing ever ... and totally friggin impossible to bloody remove without a fucking screwdriver or Stanley knife or chainsaw ... (okay maybe I exaggerated a tad on the last one)!

Nope, the life experiences of an orange and its preservation of its testicles is indeed a tough and arduous road to walk ... err roll.

Oh, and finally ... before I sign off and go and get fitted back in my straight-jacket by the nursing staff ... I must just quickly go back to baby oranges or seeds or pips. Now how come there's pips in every orange – I mean if there's lady oranges and men oranges – then what sort of weird biological freak of nature's science is going on here? Surely this must just be a heinous Dr Frankenstein-esque screw up of nature where both male and female oranges have dicks and vaginas. Are oranges hermaphrodites? And if not – how do they breed? I mean – have you ever seen them at it ... you know ... an orange orgy (an orangery)? Now I must admit that I've seen a few weird thighs (meant to type 'things' ... but I've also seen some strange thighs as well in my time) whilst under the influence of cider – but I've never witnessed copulating fruit. Mind you, if they've each got both 'poles' and 'holes' ... then maybe they just can have sex on their own ... like err I have to make do with these days (err ... actually – please forget I just typed that last bit as it's way too much information)!

So, very finally ... I hope I've proved to you that oranges might, or indeed might not – have testicles and enlightened you as to their suffering or indeed their non-suffering! But whatever the case ... it does look like the plight of the poor man-orange's testicles is not an easy one ... but hey, at least you're now aware and sensitive to their troubled lives. So please, remember that the next time you quench your thirst with a long cool glass of orange juice, if it's the 'non-smooth' variety ... then that's the oranges' bollox your rinsing over your tongue! Oh and if you're biting into a tasty freshly peeled orange

21

... please just be careful where you sink your teeth ... a bite on the nuts is truly excruciatingly painful ... even to an orange!

Discombobulated Eskimo Starfish and Flip-flops!

I'm sitting here thinking, 'Shall I start off with some sensible meaningful stuff this week to prove I'm not a total "loon" and thus demonstrate my intellectual side?' But you know what ... I'm suddenly overcome with a burning and unquenchable thirst to stomp off on a crazy random rambling nonsense rant!

So here it's comes – no thought, no sense, no rationale and no structure – just ... typed as it pops into my tiny little (but somewhat intellectual – see previous paragraph) brain! So hold on, sit comfortably, batten down the hatches (particularly if you're reading this whilst sitting on a boat in the middle of the ocean) – and I'll unleash the 'beast'!

Now I haven't been on a bus for years. I don't know why really – although I suppose having a car has got something to do with it. I should though as they're mainly double-deckers buses over here which means you can sit upstairs and see everything! Yup ... the whole god damn world (well the 35-mile-long x 15-mile-wide world that is my tiny little windswept rock of a country), which is just so important and of great interest to me as I'm a real nosey bugger. Really nosey!

Perched upstairs, you can have a good old skeet ('quick look') or gawp ('longer look') over people's walls and hedges and into their gardens. You can see them sunbathing in their gardens and even the 'produce' of their washing machines on their washing lines – not that I'm interested in seeing other people clothes hanging up drying in the breeze of course … well okay, no more than everyone else is. Actually whilst I can hand on heart (well on my chest over my heart as actually placing my hand on that particular organ – would be dangerous) confirm that I'm not interested in observing other people's clothes – I've kinda got to admit to having more than a passing interest in spying their 'smalls' airing and swinging in the wind. Mind you – only ladies that is as I've got no interest whatsoever in viewing other men's 'Boxers' and 'Y-fronts' dry, drying or still wringing wet! Oh and very quickly on this particular topic (no really) – a strange thing happened last weekend as I ambled past the washing machine. I noticed that it was making a really strange noise … like it was actually laughing. So I peered in through the big round (why are they always that shape) window on the front of our Zanussi/Hitachi/Whirlpool (they all look alike) and saw that it was busy cleaning mine and the missus's knickers. It was then that its apparent amusement was due to the fact that it was taking the piss out of our underwear!

Now – oh how I love a good old nose – not my own mind, as that's a beautiful young nose, but a 'nose' as in having a prolonged gander (skeet/gawp/look – Jesus … how many words have we silly rock-dwelling people got for having a nose)? Mind you – and referring back to my nose I'm really proud of it … but then I should be I suppose as I picked it myself!

We are a really nosey race though, us Manx (the collective name for the indigenous inhabitants of the windswept-rain-lashed rock I hail from) and are always sticking our noses into other people's business. It actually should be called the Isle of Women as we're so freaking nosey … and everyone knows that the 'females of the species' are 'busy-bodies' or 'nosey-parkers' … not you of course though … if you're a female fan of this work reading this … perish the thought. Oh and oddly enough there's actually more women in the Isle of Man than men (a reason for a country name change perhaps) … so no wonder all Manx men are 'hen-pecked' by women! Yup we Manx blokes are simply outnumbered – the fucking place is blooming overrun with freaking women.

Now whilst that might sound like a bloke's paradise on earth, like an *'If Carlsberg did Countries'* … it ain't! Women are inherently bossy. Particularly the Viking type we have here. Yup bossy women … that's a fact, I mean take me for an example – well my wife actually as I'm a man (really). My wife's the boss and I know my place … and it ain't in the bosses' seat. Oh no – she's like a frigging household dictator! Oh yeah! She's the boss alright and she's in total control. She always has complete ownership of the TV remote control and of course loves watching 'medical' and 'cookery' and 'costume drama' type programs, like all women do … and never the bloody football or any sport (Netball isn't a sport – it's just a load of silly short skirted butch ladies dicking about with a ball and a hoop). And sometimes I'll be sitting there minding my own business watching the Telly and she'll come into the lounge and utter those seemingly innocent but instructional words with that on the face of it hidden, but actually all too clear meaning … "Are you watching this!" She's not asking mind (hence no question mark) – oh no, it's a covert command that this program I'm watching is about to come an abrupt end. To be fair though, sometimes she's not so cryptic and will just sit down in 'her chair' and say lovingly (err), "Pass us the TV remote control then, you useless twat!"

Also, and like all women – she likes to spoil the fun things us men enjoy – steady now though as this is the clean-ish mail this week. It's not deliberate thigh (oops typo) 'though' – it's just an in-built 'controlling by spoiling' behavioural mechanism that all women possess. An example of this is her habit of telling me non-important and girlie gossip whilst I'm trying to watch something 'man-interesting' on TV, on the rare occasions I'm allowed to. She'll start rabbiting on about fashion or what the neighbours are up to, or just some other random and totally pointless inane bollox! Oh how I really just wanna just say, "Will you please wind your neck in my love and shut the fuck up for once in your frigging life?" … but I value my testicles too much … and like where they're currently positioned on my body!

She's also got that REALLY (caps used there for emphasis effect) female annoying habit of ruining films we're watching by blabbing out half way through – what happens at the bloody end! It's like when we were watching Titanic the other night and she's blurts out – "It sinks in the end you know!" Frig me – well that spoilt that one for me. And a while back we were happily watching that epic flick 'Jesus of Nazareth', (not that we're really into religious stuff – but, but there was a bit of gore and action in it to make it semi-watchable)

When all of a sudden (and for no apparent reason) she pipes up halfway through, "You know he dies at the end!" Well fuck me standing up – I never saw that coming … arghh – movie ruined.

Oh – and whilst we're talking about the Titanic … it was reported this week that Irish divers visiting the wreck of the Titanic said they were amazed to find that the swimming pool was still full of water!

Hgg24%%^}?bdteeaaw.45#outfikjh ((42$8$(;;66((62&9fhkirxbllloudcbhjb:#%#f:2$?ghdcb … whoops sorry about that … that crazy puppy Smudge just jumped up on me and nudged me hand and made me type illegible bollox (or perhaps 'more' illegible bollox).

But hey, the 'trouble and strife' (wife) isn't all bad. She bought me a nice new jumper this week made out of virgin wool. You know what … I never knew virgin wool came from ugly sheep!

Oh – and I had to go to the dentist this week for a filling … scary-bears or what! Now you're probably thinking – the dentist is no big drama. Well it is for me. I'm really afraid of my dentist, petrified! Mind you, the fact that he's an ex-convicted axe murderer probably has something to do with it. Still it's only twice a year that I have to go so it's not too bad I suppose – and hey there's always the added benefit that you get to read those random and crazy, way-out-there and uninteresting' magazines that you would not normally even entertain by means of cursory glance. I mean whilst you're sitting there in the dentist's waiting room, trembling like a nervous wreck and waiting the usual hour or more – that the white teethed fucker takes to actually see you – you can peruse such random gems as the National Geographic or Cosmopolitan or Good Cat Grooming Quarterly! I mean you would normally never ever, ever otherwise read this sort of absolute rubbish! Oh and hey, and why are dentist's receptionists so fucking grumpy, abrupt and ugly. My one's about as friendly as a piranha with period pains and has got a boat (face) like a bulldog chewing a wasp that another wasp had just pissed on!

Anyhow that's about me for now and I suppose I'd better sign off and get back to work … my passengers are starting to get agitated now and probably want me to get the bus moving again.

Egg On the Head, Horse in Bed, Bread!

They appear harmless enough and very laid back, as most ungulates do to be fair … or fare – if you're just about to get on a bus. Now at this point of this latest nonsense I've still got your attention – so your brain, being still switched to 'functioning mode' – will be screaming inside your head … 'What the fuck's an "ungulate" when it's at home … or somewhere else?' Well fear ye not, as you don't need to ask Mr Google … or his flippant younger brother Mr Bing or even the cleverer and more to the point cousin – Mr Wikipedia. Nope … as I'm actually gonna spill. Now an 'ungulate' is the proper name for any animal that has hooves, or in other words big toenails for feet – instead of feet or shoes! You know – like a zebra, or a goat, or a pig, or a camel or even a cat … well okay – but only if it's riding a horse, which wouldn't be a great idea would it? I mean it would truly be (you're gonna groan) a 'cathorse-trophie'! I'll get my coat!

Now where was I … oh yes, sheep? Yeah … sheep. Now I know I haven't mentioned Sheep before in this rant (although thrice now in quick succession) but that's what I was going to lead into when I started off this pathetic excuse for a short, but amusing story just before with those mentions of 'harmless' and 'very laid back'.

Well, a sheep of course is an ungulate and likewise – sheep are ungulates … 'cos these woolly backed fuckers have the same name in singular and plural form, which frankly – and just like 'fish' is a total swizz and complete laziness. I mean why not another word for the plural … it's not like there's a tax on frigging words is there!

So sheep …

Have you ever wondered what would happen if Sheep smoked grass rather than ate it? Now 'grass' that is and not 'it', as it's not practical or possible to eat 'it' as it's just a word. Mind you there is that old saying 'made to eat your words' – but hey let's face it, that's ridiculous as it's a well-known fact that words aren't actually edible – they're tasteless and not very high in protein or nutrients. Nope, in fact even the big meaty words like 'palindrome', which of course everyone's favourites are mum, dad, tit and poop, aren't high in calories. Now luckily for you I've covered 'eating words' in a previous rant – or if you haven't read that one at this juncture <<intellectual word simply meaning 'point', word – Alert>> then I'll rephrase that as – 'I've covered "eating words" in a future rant'. So I'd best move quickly back to sheep as covering that 'word eating' topic again would be about as much use as a handbrake on a canoe. Oh hang about though – and taking (meant to type 'talking' there … and I really must buy a set of smaller fingers or a tablet with massive 'fuck-off' sized keys) of words that read the same backwards as well as forwards, aka – our new good friend – 'palindrome' – there are actually lots and lots of these crazy little buggers out there in everyday use. No really. So as such I feel it would be very rude for us not explore the world of backwards-forwards words a little

... I know you wanna ... well, I know I do ... so surely that counts. And anyhow – it's still kinda 'on-(sheep)-piste' as a female sheep is one. It is Ewe know ... (groan 2).

So let's take a quick peek ... at some cheeky little Palindromes. Well there's:

- Race car ... backwards – its race caR ... but oddly enough with a little 'r' to start and a big 'R' to end ... oh and its two words ... ... which is a bit shit really if I'm honest?

And of course there's:

- Civic.

- Level.

- Sexes.

- Radar.

- Madam.

My favourite though is 'rotavator'. You know ... a mechanical soil tiller. Now I haven't got one alas – as we've no room in our garage as it's already full to bursting with random stuff like rusty old bicycles, tins of half used paint, empty gas bottles (we frigging well use oil?) and bags of cement that have gone hard! But I do so love the device and often dream about prancing around naked in our garden, like a pirouetting ballerina and with my hands grasped firmly around my throbbing tiller ... err! Maybe! So and moving on very, very quickly – can I just mention that these crafty, but clever words also occasionally get together, copulate and have offspring to form little families of back-to-front-front-to-back phrases or sentences. No really. I mean you need look no further than these following lil' beauties:

- A man, a plan, a canal: Panama.

- Dammit, I'm mad.

- As I pee, sir, I see Pisa.

- Eva, can I stab bats in a cave.

- Flee to me, remote elf.

- Rats live on no evil star.

Impressive eh? And did you get them? Well it all looks so very clever doesn't it – but you know what … this literacy shite is just that … complete shite. I mean the word that means words that's read the same backwards as well as forwards isn't freaking one … you know – a palindrome. Oh no, and therefore what complete fucking bollox a palindrome is! The freaking word's a word-fraud … or a 'frword' <<yup, a blatant applying of smartistic license and making up a new word, word – Alert>>. I mean 'palindrome' backwards it's 'emordnilap' … which is even more nonsense than this – err nonsense! Oh and very finally – this crappy word actually comes from two Greek words – Palin (again) and Dromus (run) … which is – yes you've guessed – just bollox as neither of them (in Greek or flipping English) are palindromes either!

So anyhow – and apologies for those previous paragraphs of pap (another one … sorry), let's finally move on to sheep smoking grass. Ever thought about that little scenario much … well have you? Probably not – bug ('but' even) guess what … I have. Oh yeah … and quite a lot … well since the start of this rant anyhow! Now at this moment in time you're thinking – 'Oh shit … this lame brained excuse for a short story writer is gonna run off at the mouth (and without any proper thought) about sheep smoking grass'. In other words –

you'll be thinking that you're now gonna have to endure umpteen paragraphs of piffle which will amount to a worst nightmare … or at least a fairly scary one.

Well no, as luckily for you this is a frankly ridiculous subject question to enquire as to whether you'd ever pondered … as alas the facts speak for themselves. I mean, a) sheep can't roll grass to make cigarettes as they've got hooves and no fingers, b) they can't use matches or lighters to light them with as again – they've got hooves and no fingers – have you ever tried lighting a match with your feet whilst wearing boxing gloves on them? (I have – it's tough … although that's for another rant … maybe), c) even if they could accomplish a) and b) – they wouldn't be able to pick them up to smoke them … and most importantly, d) they'd be a friggin fire hazard as it would be like you smoking with your hands tied behind your back whilst wearing a smelly fur-coat! Oh – and to compound matters and add to my further rants-writing woes … the end of my typing finger pencil is nearly blunt now (and my finger pencil sharpener is at the ironmongers (whatever happened to those guys?) getting sharpened … and won't be back till next week.

So I'd better wind this down and therefore remember … if you're ever out and about for a nice peaceful stroll in the countryside on a balmy summer's evening and you happen upon a flock of sheep and they look a bit lethargic, unsteady on their feet, wide eyed and are slurring their baas and bleats … please don't be alarmed or intimidated. Oh no. They won't in fact be stoned and high on a Class 'Hay' substance like 'whacky-backy', or about to gang up and mug you to feed their habit. Nope – they'll just be sheep being sheep, you know, ungulates – minding their own business and enjoying their daily 'score' of weed ... err I mean grass ... although grass is a weed ... hmm!

So finally on that note ... I'll sign off this rant and go and meet a good buddy of mine who just got really lucky in a competition where the 1st prize was a brand new Japanese car ...

He won a Toyota now, eh.

Frocks, Clocks, and Mr Spock's Socks?

And there's a thing … what the friggin hell's going on over at the Boston Red Socks … eh? Oh, and before I go on to vent my spleen (and I will) about a complete pile of shite (it will be) … I must just very quickly (it won't be) apologize as I've just spotted my deliberate mistake as it should be the Red 'Sox'!

Now when I said deliberate – I'm actually not meaning to criticize or scold a delicatessen (you might need to briefly deconstruct the word 'deliberate' there … or maybe not) but I just had to reflect on the crazy and frankly meaningless misspelling of the word for gloves we wear on our feet. Well okay – maybe not gloves as they've got fingers and socks haven't – and nor have Six (see even my spell check don't rate this pooh as I meant 'Sox') so I actually should've referred to 'mitts we wear on our feet' as mittens (same as mitts just longer) don't have fingers … like Sox … socks … err? And so, and yes … its hands-up time … as I actually did misspell this apparent, but not, Boston footwear on purpose to highlight its total and complete pointless (yup they're not very good) stupidity!

I mean how freaking ridiculous is that … naming a sports team (we'll be coming back to that) after an item of clothing! And not only that, but a garment <<old

fashioned word simply meaning clothes, word – Alert>>
that's worn on your smelly sweaty feet! Sounds shite?
Well that's 'cos it is just that … complete and utter shite!
Ant (typed 'And' there … but hey … we're amongst
friends) even worse still is that these so-called sporting
buffoons actually used to wear red stockings (yes girly
hosiery) whilst playing their quite frankly futile little
game.

Oh – and before I forget (as I've got the memory of
an aging goldfish with fin-rot), the mention of socks in
both the title and the 1st sentence of a rant, is both purely
coincidental and totally unusual for even for someone as
unusual as me … and I'm odder than the number seven
and as mad as a box of assorted frogs with scurvy! Do
frogs get scurvy? Anyway and moving on. Now I'm not
really sure whether our pointy-eared-oh-so logical alien
friend ('Spock' the wearer of said socks in the title) was
actually a Red Sox or in fact a baseball (BTW … that's
the err … game they play … in case you've never heard
of 'em … and you'd be easily forgiven if you ain't) fan,
as I'm not sure they play baseball on Vulcan? And if
they did, surely old Spocky-Wocky-Socky (as his
Vulcanized mates called him) would surely have been a
supporter of 'Vulcan City Space Sox' … or something
equally as similar or ridiculous … I'll bet!

And talking of old Mr Spock and his under-'foot'-
wear, which is what socks really are (like underpants for
feet), I'm actually not sure if he actually ever wore any
(socks that is and not underpants … although I'm not
sure about those either). I mean although my memory's a
bit fudged these days … I think he and all his Star Trek
chums all wore kinky black leather boots. That said, and
as my over kinky mind thinks about sexy black boots all
the time – I might just have imagined that in one of my

nightly 'wet-dreams' … err forget that last bit please as definitely a 'way too much information' moment.

And so – back to stockings. Now you might think I'm talking out of my bum-hole here (I'm not … but believe me I can as my ass can be very vocal) but they really did unbelievably wear them. And even worse – these bunch of burly sportsmen (they're not) incredibly even used to openly and proudly (I'll bet) call themselves the Boston Red Stockings! I shit you not! Now I might've perhaps (and it's a bit of a 'big ask' perhaps) understood it if they'd have called themselves the 'Boston Sexy Red Stockings', or the 'New England Suspender Belts', or even the 'Massachusetts Crotchless Panties' … as that least could've, should've, would've … appealed to my erotic side, and indeed that of men and err female 'puddle jumpers'. But just Red Stockings … what the fuck was that all about … eh? I mean it's certainly not a macho name and neither was it a very sensual <<longer word for sexy, word – Alert>> title for a sports team – if that's indeed how they were attempting to portray themselves. I'd even go as far as to say that it was simply just plain weird … just like the stupid game.

Oh and before you think that you just may as well switch over to another 'rant channel' as this one's all about stupid Baseball … fear not. No indeed … as although this one is sport orientated in parts – you can be rest assured that I'm gonna once again go completely off on a tangent <<not a word meaning a bloke who's been out in the sun, word – Alert>> anytime sooo … now! Yup – although this is just coming from my hip (not really though as that be too bonkers even for a weirdo like me) – I know I'm gonna digress and go off on a ramble …

And therefore, and quickly (maybe) going back to feet – or down to feet as that's where they live ... why oh why do they have to be so fucking ugly? I mean they're not great to look at are they ... and are in fact even more unattractive than the most unattractive human appendage <<not a word to describe an elderly ink-filled writing implement, word – Alert>> ... the male penis! Well that, and its between the legs bedfellow – the scrotum. I mean what the fuck was God thinking of when he created a bloke's 'stack' and 'sack'? Was he just having a complete giraffe or did he simply not have the foggiest idea whatsoever what the fuck they were supposed to have looked like? And if the former ... why was he taking the piss – when surely he had had an unattractive set of his own, and if the latter ... how come he didn't have a clue what they looked like ... eh? Did he not have a set of his own and if not – was he actually a she?

Hang about though – I've just realized what I just said ... which actually (and it'll come as no surprise) doesn't make sense. I mean if the penis (and its accompanying 'postman's bag') is the least good looking part of the human anatomy – then why did I just say theat (typed 'that' there – but big friggin fingers yet again on a small keypad resulted in at least a word that rhymes with the very next one after this next bracket) feet were even more unattractive? God knows I'm such a fucking literary dunce. Mind you – please don't misunderstand my previous sentence reference to me being a 'fucking literary dunce' as an admission to me having a weirdo perversion to mindlessly shagging books on stupidity. Oh no, as a) books 'don't float my boat' and b) how would you achieve this act of fornication unless of course you had a really big book ... or a really small cock! Caution though – it certainly doesn't work vice-versa, i.e. big cock small book ... not that I've tried it.

Oh and when I said that feet live 'down' there, back there – that should in fact have been qualified a bit to explain that, that is unless you live in that crazy upside down country/island/continent ... err county Australia ... where, as every schoolboy knows ... everything is upside down! Yup if you live in Oz ... your feet are 'up' and your head is down. Basically in Australia, although they don't know it, they're all actually living their lives standing on their heads! Now are this very point I'm so very much toying with the idea of ranting a fair bit about the ridiculous country that is Australia ... but d'ya know what – I'm now gonna dedicate a whole rant to the place where hats with corks on strings is the national dress and all men are called Bruce and all women Sheila.

And ... going back to the earlier mention of socks being underwear for feet, and please bear (or 'bare') with me here ... as this nonsensical nightmare should end sometime soon(ish) ... honest. Now surely they must be mustn't they (does that last bit read right to you?) as you don't usually walk around in just your socks, do you ... just like you don't swan around in just your underpants. Indeed not, as you protect your feet-modesty with shoes ... just like you cover your knickers with trousers or a skirt (if you're a 'lady-lady' ... or a jock). Or perhaps sandals – but only if you're either seriously untrendy or maybe a bit of a sock exhibitionist ... as these items of unfashionable summer footwear are pretty scantily made and as such leave little to the 'sock-modesty' imagination!

So finally (I hope as I'm getting a wee bit tired) before I actually do revert back to that nonsense weirdo American bat/ball game – I must just share this little observation I noted only the other night when incredibly (as I was dropping off to sleep) I heard my dick and feet chatting each other! I shit you not and this is how it went. One of my feet (the other one must've been asleep) moaned to my cock ... *"Poor fucking me, my days are terrible – I'm stuffed inside a smelly sock, then a sweaty shoe and am then made to walk around all day for miles!"*

"So fucking what!" said my cock, exasperated. *"That's nothing – I have to spend every day packed inside a two-sizes-too small pair of fart filled underpants and then at night I'm forced to stand to attention and then shoved head first into stinky fish smelling dark damp room and made to press-ups until I'm sick!"*

Err ... and so very quickly back to baseball as that last joke was about as funny as a bee-sting on your bell-end ... and see, I said that this nonsense wasn't going to be solely focused on sport. And indeed it hasn't been ... as only now, and at this very late-ish stage, am I gonna finally go back to the stupid American game with the bonkers tubular shaped bat.

Now you might think that to give fact based comments about baseball, I must have to be an absolute authoritative expert in the non-ball-hitting-friendly-shaped-bat game. But you'd be wrong. Indeed, as I'm just gonna base (but not ball) this rant on what I believe baseball is all about ... which in my defence is virtually the sum total of fuck all! You'll no doubt find this out from here on in. So therefore I'm gonna spout from the hip (again ... and again not really) and as such just go ahead and let lose 5 pints worth of finger ink about this bollsox (see what I did there) game.

And so baseball. Is it really, truly, deeply a sport, or just another version of that totally stupid English waste-of-time-pastime game cricket, which is not really a sport at all. I mean these white clothed posh talking (except the Aussies who also play the game but talk in a ridiculous twang that makes even American English sound sensible … which it's not) fuckers stop playing when it rains, stop for tea … and when the light starts to fade. I mean WTF … have these useless twats never heard of the fucking lightbulb and floodlights? Wankers!

I mean baseball is really nothing more than a regional game that's only popular in US and Japan – where it's known as Basai-Ballwazaki … (maybe). Oh and of course Canada where it's also most definitely played (I think … err, maybe). Now I'm not going to expand on Japanese here or indeed it's equally silly cousin Chinese. Nope I'm going to have to schedule (oh look at professional old organized me) a future rat ('rant' … red wine kicking in) about both these silly languages that no fucker outside of the few people that actually live there understand. I mean c'mon Chairman Mao – bleeding symbols for letters … what were you freaking thinking about? And I'm not sure why the Japanese copied this scribbled nonsense and just added a few extra squiggly bits to try and mask their blatant copycat fraud.

Now I'm not trying to have a go here at these Far Eastern languages in isolation, but at least the crazy French and their pathetic back to front language (it's 'Gaz's car' not 'the car of Gaz' – you fools) is written in (albeit) copied English style letters. As is the absurdly abrupt German – which just shouts at you with loud abrasive and abusive sounding words like 'FEUERZEUG' – which simply means 'lighter'. Oh yeah 'LIGHTER' … roar!? Oh and I'm not even going to take the slightest peek at Russian, as that even worse than German, is written in crazy symbols and screams at you in big signs from the top of buildings. Why oh why (one 'why' would probably have sufficed there) do the Russians feel the need to put the name of a public building in 20-foot-high red letters on its blooming roof – shouting at you … like 'Железнодорожная станция' (Railway Station) … do they all have poor eyesight?

Anyhow – when I mentioned the limited 'appeal' of Baseball what the fuckin hell (they probably do … I hope so as that's where I'll be going) is going on with the fraudulently entitled 'World Series'? Are these Americans having a complete 'Turkish? I mean there's only one country plays in this so called 'World Series' – them-fucking-selves! Why don't think they let the 'Japs' play in this 'Small-World-Series' – although I could be wrong as remember – the reality of the situation here is – is that I know little about this nonsense.

I mean what a conceited and deluded bunch of hand-pumping (think about that one – and a clenched fist around an organ of delight) these so-called sports people must be. Well okay … so maybe they also include their ridiculous moose worshipping cousins the Canadians in this frivolous <<great word … and please tell us what it actually means, word – Alert>> and bizarrely entitled sporting event. But it's hardly the world – is it? And anyhow can you even count Canada's inclusion – if indeed they actually are playing this cricket-perversion, which as I've already mentioned is itself a pile of pointless English wank (although I'm not referring to the flop-haired-plum-voiced actor 'Hugh Grant' in that last bit). I mean Canada's not even a real place is it – it's just populated by a load of ancient Brits and Frogs who couldn't read their sea charts and ended up run aground about 500 miles north of where they wanted to be – in New York. And once they'd realized they were in Canada they were too stupid to be able to read any maps they possessed to enable them to get back to the good ole US of A.

Mind you the word 'Maps' is 'Spam' backwards so maybe it wasn't all their stupid fault as just a very early form of hacking by the map makers who deliberately sabotaged their geographical etchings as so to ensure these clearly clueless Anglo-Franco twerps got lost … and didn't end up populating the United States with simpletons (hmm … maybe not all of them got lost). I mean Canada … it's a bit of a joke really ain't it. Are they English or are they Froggish? The truth is that they can't really make their minds up. Now I've been to Canada countless times … well okay, make that zero-times – but you can just tell that they're odd. Just look at their capital city … its named after a cheap excuse for a Beaver … that probably stowed away from England and itself got lost. Canadians … more friggin' like 'Can't-Americans' as the reality of the situation is that they're simply wannabe Americans who don't wanna be Americans.

And so very finally back to the 'Red Sox'. Why not the 'Boston Bravehearts', the 'Boston Brawn', the 'Boston Ballistic' … or something else more bloody macho. But freaking socks … sorry 'Sox' … the stupid game playing looneys can't even spell. And anyhow, socks … who the fuck do theses 'New England (it's not is just a freezing sparsely populated North-Western territory in America – that like the rest of the daft country couldn't make up their own unique name for where they friggin live) imbeciles think they are – Harry Potter's friggin 'Dobby'. Wankers! I mean with this

43

dumber than dumb ass mentality what the friggin heck do they call their undies then eh ... Knicks? Err ... actually they do ... although we really shouldn't believe anything that the New York Knickerbockers basketball (err ... I meant baseball – but hey, that hoop loving nonsense is complete tomfoolery shite too) team say ... what, with such a totally ridiculous and frankly twattish name like that.

Oh, and I suppose we'd better very finally (before both you and I die of baseball boredom – just like you would if you ever had to freaking watch a game) quickly look at some of the ridiculous team names of this oh so ridiculous and so-called sport. A sport that's played on a fringing triangle-shaped pitch by blokes wearing with silly cheap plastic hats! Well okay maybe the 'comedy' hats cost a few quid each and perhaps the playing field has a couple more right angles. So anyway ... the (ahem) teams ...

The 'Minnesota Twins' – Eh? Surely there's more than two of them in the friggin stupid team and are they identical? If not ... then why 'Twins'? Does Arnold Schwarzenegger and Danny De-freaking-Vito play for them? No, do they fuck. The liars and Great Lake losers (err – I hope Minneapolis – named after a daft cartoon mouse on holiday in Athens – is near these oversized US puddles).

The 'Kansas City Royals' – does the Queen even know where this cow loving dust bowl is – let alone having ever visited there? No, of course she doesn't. Royals my frigging ass ... I mean what's friggin royal about Kansas City? And anyhow – there's friggin two of them in different states. Hey maybe they should hook up with their cross-river city friends and call themselves the 'Twins' ... err no ... that already been done.

The 'Pittsburgh Pirates' – the stupid city is like a million miles away from the ocean – so pirates of friggin what? Metal working? Whoo … that's freaking scary and has every landlubber-sailor shitting their non-nautical-pants … I'll bet. Unless of course they're just Johnny Depp fixated fuckwit-wannabes! Ridiculous.

The 'Los Angeles Dodgers' – what exactly are they trying to 'avoid' … eh? Pitched balls? No wonder they've been so completely shite since they upsticked from Brooklyn – which is just the most chicken shit and selfish thing any sports team could ever do. I mean did all their fans have to move from gloomy old New York to sunny LA? No. Total tosh.

The 'Los Angeles Angels' – what a freaking mega-yawn this is as all these unimaginative 'living in their "Dodging" tosspots neighbour's shadow' have done is simply repeat their city name and drop an 'e'. Grrr …

The 'Cleveland Indians' – now I've been to Cleveland many a time and never have I been chased down the high streets by a man on a horse with a bow and arrow and a tomahawk screaming "Whoo-ooh-whoo-ooh". Mind you – I've kinda gotta admit that like Canada, I've in fact never actually been to Cleveland … but in my defence I have been to New Orleans – and whilst there I never felt threatened of attack by a painted face man with a big chopper. Although there was this one boozy night on Bourbon Street – when … err … well that's for another time.

The 'St. Louis Cardinals' – they're not. Nope, these delusional ecclesiastical wannabes aren't even lowly vicars or priests let alone higher status 'bible-bashers'!

The 'Tampa Bay Rays' – I mean c'mon lads think of something a bit more original than just a random word that rhymes with the last stupid name of the stupid place. Unless of course it's just total conceited bragging that these lucky fuckers live somewhere where the sun shines more than twice a fucking year – like here in the Isle of Man. Christ … if we had a baseball team (which we haven't as we've got better things to do with our spare time like play dominoes or count rain) then they'd be called the 'Manx Miserable Moaners' – which at least would be factual!

And so very finally, finally … it's the 'Chicago White Sox'. WTF? I mean come on White Sucks (oops – Freudian 'big fingers typing' slip there … or maybe not) … err 'Sox' as once again they're not … they're just socks! And worse still, what a complete and utter fashion faux-pas <<French phrase – 'cos we can't think of our own, phrase – Alert>> that is. I mean white socks or friggin sox were never ever trendy, aren't currently trendy … and never ever will be friggin trendy … so get a fucking grip you 'Windy City' wankers (a possible alternative name for the team … maybe not)! I mean to have any creditability whatsoever in the wearing of white socks you'd need to be a sports team … oh hang on though! Doh … best forget what you've just read.

Abhorrent Sleeves Eat Belligerent Cheese?

Isn't it funny that words don't really mean what they say? You know 'do what it says they do on the friggin tin' … as such. Not that words come in tins mind as that would be a) freaking ridiculous and b) blooming impractical … oh and there's a cheeky little 'c' in there to add in as well … c) impossible.

Yeah, impossible and improbable (or the other way round). I mean … who would make all the tins – zillions (that's like a lot more than millions as a 'z' is a bigger letter than a 'm') of them every day – and who and how would they transport them to everybody's mouths each time they spoke. And how would they get the tins in your bloody mouth for the words to be placed in too … not through your mouth surely … as that's where they're coming out of. So therefore your arse would be the only orifice <<infrequent used word alert>> available if you were a man – and if you were a woman – then both the arse and 'fandango' (or vagina, clunge, snatch, fanny <not in the US of course where it's your arse – eh?>, camel toe, fadge, beaver, minge … and of course the two 'Lady-Taboos' for their bits <which I won't mention> – the 'T' word and the 'C' word … or 'Tuesday, Wednesday And Thursday' and 'See You Next Tuesday' … that's a slightly harder one to work out … but think about the sound of the 1st two words and the capitals). Btw … is that the longest use of brackets ever … should I be contacting those geezers at the Guinness World Records?

Mind you, in thinking about it – I suppose it would have to be the arse as that's of course where the ancient saying comes from that was invented by very sorta prehistoric people (like the Egyptians) i.e. 'talking out of one's arse'.

Now it's a very little known fact (I didn't even know it – until I thought it up just a minute ago) that this 'arse-phrase' was actually invented by those triangle loving sand dwellers – the ancient Egyptians (although some of were youthful?) 'Tis true … as although they weren't able to write properly and had a fetish for wrapping each other up in bandages and then burying themselves, these poor fuckers also didn't have the common sense to invent tins … to put words into. And therefore their words had to come from somewhere. And this of course ties in with that well-known historical fact that all ancient Egyptians actually talked out of their arses. The 'arse' of course is a modern day derivation of the Egyptian word 'Asp' – invented by Queen Cleopatra who first coined the phrase 'talking out of one's asp' – or 'snake talk' … with 'snake' of course being the ancient hieroglyphic word for bottom – erm maybe. Now that last bit was possibly the biggest pile of bullshit I've ever, ever typed … and boy, do I type a lot of cow faeces <<very under-used word for shit, word – Alert>>.

The reality was of course that Tin wasn't actually invented until the 19th century by a young explorer boy called 'Tin-Tin' … who was so very impressed by his discovery that he changed his name (from Claude

Wilfred Hinds-Froggatt) to 'Tin' … but alas he had a stutter!

Going back to those Egyptians – they were so clever in other ways though and so very instrumental in forging our development as not only did they invent words (maybe) – 'pre-tin' … or 'Pretinoric' <<new word, word – Alert>>, but they actually also taught us how to blooming walk (definitely). Now you might be scoffing at this point (or at the very first line of this e-mail), but I shit you not as I have well documented proof to support this.

Indeed. Remember the girly pop group 'The Bangles' and their greatest ever song (arguably) 'Walk like an Egyptian' … from their highly acclaimed (arguably x 2) 1985 album 'Different Light'? Well this was of course based on fact … I mean they were nice girls and wouldn't have just made the lyrics up to get and loads of dosh from some meaningless nonsense – would they?

So anyway – I've digressed a bit again … and back to words in tins. Now how would 'they' know when you were about to speak to put each word in a tin? And who the fuck are 'they'? And who would print the words on the tins and how would they know what to print or – thinking about it … what not to print – as remember – they wouldn't know what you were about to say and anyhow … don't actually mean what they say on the … err tin! Eh? And hey, what happens to all the tins after each word was 'used' – recycled or just 'canned' … excuse the pun. And quickly – before I drive you out of your tin(y) mind – what about Tinnitus – was that caused by the clanking of tins as they delivered words … err – if they ever did … err which they didn't as this bollox was just suggesting that they could've or even should've?

Anyway ... words misrepresenting themselves by having absolutely the sum total of Jack shit (did he and if so, when ... and why?) to do with what they purport <<interesting word alert>> to say. So let's finally look at a few examples that'll prove the English language is really just having a laugh. And it is you know, I mean look at the word for people who have trouble reading letters and words. Did they call it 'boop' or 'nak' or even 'foz'? Oh no. They called it 'Dyslexia'. WTF ... I can't even pronounce that and I'm a nuclear physicist (well ok ... so I run a call centre – but that's a minor point – as if I really were a nuclear physicist the I wouldn't be ... eh?). And why is one sheep a 'sheep' and 10 sheep still 'sheep' ... whatever happened to 'sheeps'? Oh and 'frogmarched' ... they blooming don't ... they just hop about a bit and swim (poorly) ... unless of course you're talking about French soldiers ... but hey, it's not politically correct to call them frogs, so I won't (even if they are 'cos they eat them)!

Oops – so back to those examples to prove that I'm not just standing here with my back to you, bent over touching my toes and with my trousers and knickers around my ankles – or in other words – talking through my fooking arse! So – before you die of old age ... let's finally freaking look at some of these misleading words that clearly don't do what they say on the err ... tin:

1. Carpet: not a vehicle driven by a domesticated animal?

2. Wallet: not a partitioning structure with a cute little alien (who rides a bike) leaning against it?

3. Cupboard: not a drinking vessel made out of a thin piece of wood?

4. Yard; it's not – its way bigger … ours is about 150 feet?

5. Hammock: not a joint of meat that you make fun of?

6. Sink: well ours doesn't, it just sits there?

7. Canteen: not a capable young adult?

8. Converse: not prison poetry?

9. Legend: not another word for your foot?

10. Innovation: not applause in a pub?

11. Abundance: not a bread boogie?

12. Adamant: not the first insect?

13. Antelope: not a quick insect marriage?

14. Carnation: not the United States?

15. Nightmare: not a dark horse?

16. Headlines: not face wrinkles?

17. Triumphant: not a winning insect?

18. Parole: not fatherhood?

19. Shamrock: not a fake diamond?

20. Seething: not an eyeball?

And of course,

21. Thinking: not a skinny monarch?

So there you have it really … that's this particular Pantsrantian in a nutshell … and not a tin. Hmm … maybe I should've actually started off in that 'nut container' direction at the beginning of this dross and as such not wasted one thousand three hundred and six words on weird words and words in tins. Actually make that 1,310 words now … err 1,311 … shit I'm gonna stop looking at that Word Count counter thingamajig at the bottom left of my screen as it's just going up and up and I'm not at all sure how to make it stop. Actually though (and I'm over 1,350 now) I've just had a possibly crazy but perhaps super-simple idea that could bring an abrupt halt to this growing never ending story! Instead of making more words (see … I'm at 1,385 now) by thinking and typing complete shite – why don't I just eat my words!

Alternative Carparks Wield Untransferable Skylarks?

Well … and no not a place where you find drinking water lying at the bottom of a hole – but a word that means 'and so'. So <<and nope, not a 'delete repeated word' – Alert … and anyhow the 2nd one's starts with a capital 'S'>> isn't it so truly and awesomely amazing that some (actually quite a lot) words – have two meanings. Why is this? I mean it's not like there's a tax on words is there? And abutting (actually typed 'anyhow' there) if there was – who the freak would pay it, regulate it, enforce it and reconcile it. Eh? No-one, that's who – or not as no-one is actually no-one … Err?

Anyhow – I'm in danger of disappearing up my own ass here and finding the long lost treasures of Babylon … if there were any … and anyhow what would they be doing hiding up my back door orifice? Although that said … in reality, there could lots of stuff hiding up my derriere <<let's try to pretend to speak French, word – Alert>> – but do we really wanna go there … I mean talk about it and not actually go and have an ass inspection.

So, swiftly – back to words with two meanings – that are of course spelt the same … as there are others that aren't – like 'flower' and 'flour' … which (witch) are not – and which mean different things. One's a plant and the other's made out of a plant … hmm!

Like the word flat … I mean that word is just having a blinking 'Turkish'. Isn't it! Is it a low ceilinged <<doesn't look correct, but is, word – Alert>> apartment-like place to live or something lying down without much depth? Who knows – and quite frankly who cares – but why just one word – why not two. I mean couldn't we just call the apartment one – a 'Flat' and the object lying face (or backside) down one a 'Flin' … you know – a merging of the words flat and thin? Hey don't scoff – it's a plausible <<a word that should be used more to make you sound clever – Alert>> idea.

Mind you – I suppose I could muddy the waters here a bit and add that we could call the apartment one a 'flatulent' … but only if you were renting it – you know … borrowing it i.e. a flat you'd 'lent'! Okay maybe not! And anyhow what about if you'd bought your apartment flat? Nope the 'flatulent' idea really stinks … which of course it would!

Then there's 'duck'. A water loving feathered bird (aren't they all) that Walt Disney had a fetish about or, meaning to take action to get out of the way by lowering oneself nearer to the ground to avoid being twatted by an incoming projectile <<love that as it sounds like it means, word – Alert>>

Oh and let's not forget the crazy word 'spell'. This one's a real mind fucker as it has 3 meanings, (i) to put letters in the correct order to write an actual meaningful word, (ii) or a period of time (I won't do the word 'period'), or (iii) what that specie-four-eyed-twonk Harry Potter dies when he's either a) pissed off, b) wants something without having to do much, or is just pissassing around with his conical hat and cloak wearing mates, with his stiff wand grasped firmly in his hand (steady)!

Then there's the word 'pop'. Now is this a fizzy drink that doesn't render <<love that not used enough, word – Alert>> one to be inebriated <<great alternative to pissed, word – Alert>> or another name for your old man – your dad?

And what about the pretty ridiculous word … err 'pretty'. This silly multi used word can mean 'fairly' – as in, 'that's a pretty tough thing to do' … and of course, some chick, (not a hen though as that'd be ridiculous) but a female or an object that was beautiful … like a chick … err I mean bird … err I mean lady!

Oh – and what about Turkey – well that's for another day as something I mentioned earlier has just gnawed <<stupidly spelt … but an actual word – Alert>> through into my thought train.

Oh … ("Oh no," I hear you groan) … I must, and I really 'mean' (another two meaning word as … err … meaning 'explain' or really 'frugal' … oh and of course 'unkind' … so that's a three-er) must go back to the (and on the face of it) inexplicable use of the word 'Turkish'! Which at the time – a moment ago … or two – probably was inexplicable. Well … a 'Turkish' – is, by the way, Cockney (London) 'rhyming slang' for the word 'laugh' … i.e. a 'Turkish Bath' = a 'laugh'.

Now I think at this point it's actually worth taking a quick (I'm now lying as it'll no doubt be anything but) 'butchers' at Cockney rhyming slang … which will really, really help you out if you ever wake up one bleary-eyed morning naked and without a penny … in London … or 'Landan' as native 'Landaners' would say.

So – Cockney 'Rhyming Slang' is believed to have originated in the mid-19th century in the East End of London, with sources suggesting sometime in the 1840s – which is a long time ago even for an old fart like me! Apparently it dates from around 1840 (I've just said that … err) and among the predominantly 'Cockney' <<BTW – not a rude word meaning a bloke whose dick hangs quite low – Alert>> population of the East End of London who are well-known (honest) for having a characteristic accent and speech patterns. It remains a matter of speculation whether rhyming slang was a linguistic <<clever word for language – Alert>> accident, a game, or a cryptolect <<big intellectual word, I have no idea what it means – Alert>> developed intentionally to confuse non-locals. And yes – I deffo did get that last para from Wiki! (;0)

Anyhow – enough of that informative bollox … as that's not really my purpose in life – so let's now look (no we really must) at some examples!

Oh and before we do, firstly let's go back to 'butchers' which I mentioned a day or two ago (well it would be if you read this rubbish in bite sized chunks over the space of a few days or so – in order to retain a modicum <<Latin – aren't I a smart-ass, word – Alert>> of sanity. Well a 'butchers' … means to have a 'look' – from 'butcher's hook'. Get it! ((0) … <<oops mistyped as drunken or sleepy smiley face – Alert>> (;0)

So – a few more examples – well here we go … and you're gonna learn something this week that could save your life … but definitely won't.

Okay – and hang on as you're not going to 'Adam and Eve' it (believe) here they are:

1. 'Tom and Dick' = Sick.

2. 'Boat Race' = Face.

3. 'Syrup of Fig' = Wig.

4. 'Frog and Toad' = Road.

5. 'Loaf of Bread' = Head.

6. 'Apple and Pears' = Stairs.

7. 'Dog and Bone' = Phone.

8. 'Whistle and Flute' = Suit.

9. 'Septic Tank' = Yank.

10. 'Sky Rocket' = Pocket.

11. 'Plates of Meat' = Feet.

12. 'North and South' = Mouth.

12a. (I'm superstitious) 'Jam Jar = Car.

14. 'Currant Bun' = Sun.

15. 'Brown Bread' = Dead.

16. 'Brahms and Liszt' = Pissed.

17. 'Barney Rubble' = Trouble.

18. 'Barnet Fair' = Hair.

19. 'Brass Tacks' = Facts.

And finally before you start to 'Darby and Joan' (Moan) …

20. 'Dickie Bird' = Word.

So, there you have it – and now – I'd better quit whilst I'm ahead (I am aren't I?) as your probably about to get into a right 'two and eight' (state)!

Conical Barnacles amidst Chrome Chastised Chronicles?

Okay … so the title's a bit of a worry this week, but hey … then so am I, I s'pose <<silly shortened word – Alert>>. Now – abs severe (I actually typed 'and very' … there?) quickly … why are words shortened and even sometimes misspelt. I mean – is it for the benefit of Dwarfs with learning difficulties … or just lazy people who may be either vertically challenged or not! Or indeed both. Like … why is it that we all just have to call a 'doctor' – 'doc'? I mean it's not a hard or indeed tiring word to say – unless of course you're a rabbit called 'Bugs'. But then he's got an excuse I s'pose (grrr) … as he's a 'carrot muncher' … and it's a scientifically proven fact that whilst they can see in the dark, they've got absolutely no aptitude <<fairly rarely used word – Alert>> for being able to pronounce words of more than 5 letters! Or did I just make that up? And anyhow … after years and years of studying big thick, heavy, serious and musty (they always are) books and pictures and diagrams of naked people and their 'bits' … just to become doctors … the very least we can do is afford them the courtesy of at least addressing them by their full and correct title … 'Dr' … err, moving on!

And what about the latest (well 'latest' since about 2004) bloody annoying craze of shortening the word for that totally pointless and water-tasting fruit … the 'Apple' … to 'App' … and even worse, the grocers where you can buy them online being changed to an 'AppStore'? If this is such a big deal – why has no one bothered to shorten 'orange' to 'ora' or 'oran'? Mind you, it had a colour named after it so I suppose (didn't shorten that one that time) they can't complain … not that they could mind as they can't speak … they're fruit! Oh – and as for the misspelt shortened words – well what about 'e.g.' – for 'example'? I mean where's the bloody 'g' in 'example'? And what about the truly ridiculous shortening of the saying 'that is' to 'i.e.'! I mean where's the fooking 'e' in those two words … nowhere – that's blinking where!

Oh – and sweeping right back to talking about dwarfs with learning difficulties … never let one do your homework for you. Oh no … as it's not big and it's not clever!

Now don't even start me on 'acronyms' as that's for another future rant … and anyhow, what's the acronym for acronym? Eh! Exactly … it's all bollox!

So onto today's topic … clouds (no really).

Do you ever, like me … look up at clouds and wonder if there's UFOs hiding behind them or in them … or is that a 'just me alert'? You know … an alien life-form in its technically advanced spacecraft – camouflaged <<I love that word, but it's not very good one as you can see it, word – Alert>> and clouded' behind a – err cloud. You know … like a Klingon bird of prey's 'cloaking device', from Star Trek's … err 'Star Trek episodes. Now I'm assuming that you're familiar with Klingons? If not (and shame on you as they're real) either watch a Star Trek episode … or failing that –

simply check your underwear the morning after waking up following a heavy night on the beer and a follow-on curry. I'll bet there'll be some 'Klingons' in the gusset <<great rudimentary word, word – Alert>> of your drawers to observe – hold your nose though.

Anyhow – enough digression <<Ooh, look at me, word – Alert>> ... so let's move on to actually look at clouds. Yep – we're gonna, alas.

Now ... there are lots of different types of clouds and the really weird thing about these silly non-relevant (okay, so they might be) floating balls of cotton wool is that they've all got really weird fucking names. It's like some really mad twat (apologies for that word ... but it's typed now) thought them up whilst on day-release from the Loony-Bin, and who happened upon an Internet cafe and randomly (very randomly) typed in the word 'cloud' with his\her forehead ... or a stick ... or axe! They then went straight on to Wikipedia and added in these name references for clouds! Really ... you can trust me!

So ... what weird names? Well – we have 'cumulus' which means – 'heap' or 'pile' in Latin ... more about that shite in a moment. Then we have 'stratus' which means – 'sheet or 'layer' in ... yes you've guessed ... Latin. And let's not forget 'nimbus' which means – 'rain' or 'storm' ... in yes ... blooming Latin!

Now there are lots of different variations of these types of clouds (at least you're getting a sorta weather lesson this week out of my inane rubbish), so here are the main protagonists <<big word that hardly gets used, word – Alert>>

There's stratocumulus, altostratus, and altocumulus ... that all sound like fungi or mushrooms that you can't, but perhaps should, eat. Then there's cirrus ... that sounds like one of those 'eco-friendly' hybrid cars that only 'do-gooders' or wealthy hippies drive and then plug in to the mains – like earth saving twonks – when they get home? And let's not forget cirrocumulus, cirrostratus and nimbostratus ... which all sound like medical conditions of the kind that you wouldn't wanna publicize the fact you were suffering from. And of course there's cumulonimbus ... who discovered America! (:0)

Oh and finally let's not forget 'cucumberous' – one that looks like a saucy or inviting looking vegetable – that in reality is neither and tastes like water that a newt with a painful bladder infection has pissed in ... and it gives you gas (or a 'just me alert' again)? Hmm ... maybe there ain't a cloud type of that name after all!

So quickly back to Latin. Now why are clouds all given Latin names? What's that all about ... I mean Latin's not even a proper language – just silly words made to give stuff a bit of credibility or to look intellectual! And where the hell is 'Lat' anyhow, you know the country where 'Lat's in ... or Lat-in ... err! Can you point to it on a map? If you can ... you win a cigar! Nope. It's not a real place and so it's not a real language.

Okay – so I know you're thinking ... well, there's Latin America. Okay – there is – but why the heck do they call Latin America – Latin America? I mean no one speaks Latin in South America – they speak Portuguese and Spanish and ... err ... err ... err ... Chilean? Now I've had a rant about the inappropriately <<bloody difficult to spell word Alert>> named Chile a good while ago so I won't go back there again ... not that I've actually ever been there – but you know what I mean. Well okay I might actually go one day ... but only if I wore a jumper – as it'd be 'chilly' ... oh hang about ...

it's spelt different? Anyway … I think Latin is so bizarre and frankly ridiculous, that it needs a whole rant dedicated to itself – so that's for another day as well!

So – and finally back to clouds. Well as well as hiding alien life-forms, no doubt just waiting to invade and take over our bodies when they catch us off guard … they can also be eaten and are indeed an amazing source of sugar, trans-fats and protein! No really. Yes, indeed … as everyone knows that clouds are actually foodstuffs and made of a) marsh mallows (if they're just white fluffy ones) or b) marsh mallows that have been dropped in the dirt (and rolled a bit) – if they're storm clouds and c) candy floss if there those 'red sky at night' ones!

"It's all utter tripe and bollox" … I hear you grumble … well, maybe. But if you've never eaten a cloud … I'll wager that you don't really know what they're made of – do you! So until you do … zip it!

Oh and finally to finish on … and I better had before all our minds are 'clouded' with utter nonsense … I mustn't forget the yellowy/gold coloured ones. Well … these are simply clouds that God has taken a leak in … which has the same effect as when you pee in the snow!

Hat's Sushi Delight Forge Roof Tiles for Spite?

So … is glass good or bad?

Now before you hover (not really as remember … you're a person and can't fly … well not unaided) your trigger finger (again not really – as it's just a digit and not a gun) over the 'delete' button – this might not actually be such the incredibly ridiculous question and/or statement as you might initially think. So please bear (no you're not really – you're a person remember … and probably don't have big paws) with me and I'll either attempt to explain … or go off on one, which if I'm entirely honest, at this moment in time – I'm not really sure as to which way this will go! Mind you, I'd put my house on it being the latter … but then again when you analyse that thought process through a little bit … you'll realize that my home ain't in danger as it's just me typing this shite and therefore can decide which way it goes as my brain and finger engage. So, yeah it's the latter, but then again also the former as I'm gonna eventually go on to explain the random question that opened this pap. Oh and yes … I still get to keep my home … so unlucky suckers as my four bed (rooms, not just beds) house is mine for keeps … although you're welcome to come round and cut the lawn whenever you 'feel the urge'.

Oh now that reminds me … What's a partially mown lawn and me (and you – I'll bet) after three pints of lager got in common? We're both 'half cut'. Nowcifvyiurec (I actually typed 'now if you're not' – but my spell check was temporarily possessed by an alien with 'another planetary languages learning difficulty') familiar with the phrase 'half cut'? Well this is an old (and new) English phrase used to describe someone who is quite inebriated, or intoxicated … or just pretty pissed. I'm not by the way … well not just yet! Oh, oh … and quickly back to that awesome word for being drunk … imagine if there actually was a place … err like a town … called 'Ebriated' and you got absolutely 'wasted' there after 'horsing' down gallons of wine and beer. That would mean that you'd be inebriated in Ebriated … how funny is that, eh! Err … okay – just me … but hey – it amused my 15-watt brain. Mind you, I'm easily pleased as my brain's dimmer than a broken bulb in a power cut!

And so – and back in the real world again please Quaggers – let's swiftly revert back to 'glass'. Oh but before we do … can I quickly just flick (pretend this is like a page of a very bad book) back to wine … which I very briefly mentioned a few lines ago. Now apart from dogs and cheese and goats and me, wine is my favourite subject and drink … accepted I don't drink dogs or cheese or goats … or even me! So quickly … to wine. Now why is wine called wine and more (or less) importantly is it known as 'vino' in every single county in the world except France (where it's ridiculously called 'vin') and England (where it's laughably called 'plonk')? It is you know. Well okay, I might've oversimplified Oenology (your gonna have to google that word … or maybe not if you're a piss-head like … err me) a bit, but in my defence, if you walk into any bar absolutely anywhere in the world except 'Plonkland' and

'Frogland' ... and ask for a vino, then that's what you're served up to soak your palette. I mean if you go to America, or Australia, or Brazil, or Greenland (it's not), or Botswana, or Iceland (it is), or even friggin Legoland (again ... it is) and ask for a vino – then that's exactly what you'll be getting – a glass of the red or the white stuff. Not a drink of vin or plonk – as there's no such friggin thing.

Now the word for the study of wine is – 'oenology' (and if you didn't google it a few lines back ... you don't need to now) and was created by the founder of Wine ... the Spanish poet 'Juan Ola Gee'. Now ole – err I mean old (getting carried away with the Spanish theme) so loved his invention that he was always – yup you've guessed it ... inebriated. As such he was as pissed as fart when he came up with a title for his new drink and meant to call it 'oneology' – as wine to him was the numero 1 and he thought that adding a bit of Latin shite at the end would give it that air of 'snobbish' credibility. Additionally, he liked the fact that it kinda rhymed with his name ... which was important to old Juan, given his love of verse! But being so sloshed – he hiccupped and stumbled a bit as he wrote down the name for his new beverage at the 'New Names for Stuff Registry Office' in downtown Seville (it might've been Madrid, but hey – one Spanish town's the same as the next) and misspelt it to the frankly ridiculous word we have today.

Oh but quickly back to the Spanish town of Seville. Now although the birutgfjkosce (can you believe I actually tried to typed 'birthplace' there) of wine (maybe) the people there are probably the dumbest on the planet. I mean everyone in the whole city (bar none) are totally unable to correctly pronounce the name of the flipping place they friggin live in. I shit you not – these

65

thickets call it Sevilla! WTF … get an English dictionary you complete losers … it's blinking Seville!

Anyhow – I've just realized that I could rant about wine for days and I'm in danger of hijacking this glass focused one – the topic of which I haven't even touched on yet. Therefore, I'm gonna park wine for a future rant and 'reflect' (see what I did there) back to glass.

Oh but first – and please forgive one more little digression. Now do you remember back to the beginning of this mega-multi-off-on-a-tangent post when I mentioned trigger-finger? Oh shit … yeah you do! Well … and now I'm revisiting this phrase very briefly because it's just quite frankly stupid. I mean – how do 'they' (whoever thinks up English phrases – and I'll bet it's a group of bespectacled literary loving people called Colin and Keith and Prudence and Cynthia … yup – weirdos) know which finger is your 'trigger' one? Is it your right 'index' finger or your left one? How do 'they' flipping well know if your left or right handed? And what if you're ambidextrous? Then it would surely be your 'trigger fingers'! Oh, and why call it your 'index' finger anyhow? I mean – an 'index' tells you what stuff's all about or what's included … like in a book. Well bollox to that – as my index fingers (left or right) contain absolutely no instructions as to the rest of my fingers … like what order and position they appear in on my hand or what they actually do!

Then on this theme – but not mentioned until now is the bonkers word 'firearm'. Now at this point I'm in serious danger of totally losing the original glass plot here … but you know what – I'm gonna push the envelope a tad further … with two 'revert-backs' (a new title for my annoying habit of revisiting previous text). And so 'firearm' … what's that then? Eh? Now we all know it's a name for a gun – but surely it's a pretty crappy one as it's just a gun. I mean you don't go to a gun shop and buy a rifle or a pistol off the shelf and it's already got an upper limb attached to it has it? And reversely-perversely (ooh) your arm ain't a flipping weapon all on its own is it? I mean whilst I can make a few hurtful gestures with my arm – it can't flipping 'fire' itself off at someone – or shoot projectiles without an accompanying firearm … err I mean gun … can it?

So finally – before I go and break into glass – I really have to just go very briefly back to err 'briefly'. Now what a strange word this is as it completely doesn't do what it 'says on the tin'. I mean the Oxford (it's a book and town and not a place where bovine types cross a river) English Dictionary says this word means a 'short time' or 'fleetingly'. But nowhere is there any mention whatsoever in that silly book of words for words – of a French cheese loving insect pest – is there! Bollox that's what it is … but hey … dictionaries are gonna get a whole future rant to themselves.

And so finally – glass. Well this 'see through' substance is actually made from burnt sand … well melted sand – which is the same thing only hotter. Now everyone knows sand is yellow … so how come glass is transparent <<big word for 'you can see through' … and not a cross-dressing mum or dad, word – Alert>>. Well that's a head-wrecker in itself … but it is what it is. But that aside … is it good or bad?

Now I asked this seemingly absurd question as I was in the shower this morning and I noticed that the glass surrounding me and protecting my modesty had the word 'tempered' on it. So what does that freaking mean … is it 'good' or 'bad' tempered? I mean do you get 'bad' glass and 'good' glass … and just 'okay' … or 'mild mannered' glass? And if so – which is which … as its blooming important to know what you're getting into (literally with a shower) when you get up close and personal to our burned-sand-made 'friend' … or maybe 'fiend'. Hmm?

And why doesn't your shower glass tell you which one it is? I mean what if it's the 'bad' sort and it attacked you as you frolicked around naked in your shower – and punched you in the face … or worse, gave you a Chinese burn (why are they called that as nowhere have I seen that our oriental friends liked to twist wrists in an aggressive manner). And if it was the 'good' sort then surely it should 'sweet talk' you or even 'cuddle' you as you washed your bits. Hey – and maybe if the 'good' stuff was really that 'good' then perhaps it should even sexually 'play with you' as you soaped yourself down! Err … now maybe I'd, no 'we'd' (as we're in this shit together) better scrap that last bit gang, as amazing though glass is (as it's see-through sand … which is kinda magic) it ain't got the hands or arms that of course would be required to fondle or molest you … err, but in a endurable (typed 'pleasurable' there but let's run with it) way.

"Oh Quaggers, you silly sausage," (I'm not – I'm a human) I hear you say (the 'Oh Quaggers' bit and not the 'human' bit – as I said that) … "tempered glass doesn't describe the mood or behavioural tendencies of pieces of glass – it means it's 'safety' glass!" Do what? safety glass … what complete friggin bollox that is then. I mean, okay it might protect you from receiving a few minor cuts and scratches should your shower cubicle unexpectedly implode – or your car windscreen suddenly decide to stop its forward motion and come to a complete halt mid-highway and smack you right in face!

It might even save you from a few grazes and bruises if you tripped whilst – yup – inebriated and fell through your Irish fitted double glazing leading out into your garden – you know … your 'Paddy O' Doors'! But will it protect you in a sword fight with a highly strung samurai warrior high with a personality disorder … or other life threatening situations? Eh? I mean would it save you from a flash flood in an Amazonian rain forest on a wet weekend, or from receiving a broken left little toe whilst playing Hockey that eventually leads to your leg withering and then falling off? Or would it protect you from being mugged by a 'firearm' (yup) wielding squirrel wearing high heels and a robber's mask? Will it fuck!

Oh no – this overpriced (I'll bet – but don't actually know) sandy stuff is really only useful for one thing – looking through. I mean – that's it … It's nothing special – just a view. Well unless it's opaque <<great word, word – Alert>> and that's pretty useless as all that does is prevent you from spying on ladies (or gents) in the shower and getting your 'cheap thrills'! I for one hate opaque glass as there's nothing I like better than being a peeping Tom … even if my name's neither … err … just forget that last bit please. Actually don't … as it's just reminded me of a related funny … What's the difference between a peeping Tom and a pick pocket? One snatches watches whilst the other …!

And so … 'back in the room' … continuing on this theme (glass without a view and not spying on chicks) let's not forget our oldest 'glass' best friend (well to me they are) the mirror. Now although this very magical reflective sand that can't actually be looked through – it does provide a good view. Well I suppose that's dependent on who's looking in it, or if it's you – then whether or not you just got up out of bed! I know they never let me down … but then hey – it's hardly like I have to worry about a hair being out of place is it! But are they good or bad? I suppose that's the result of what you see when you look into one … I mean if you look like a swan (although not literally as that would be just weird) then it's a good mirror with good glass, but if you look like shit … then it's a 'bad-ass glass!

One thing though – although mirrors are very clever devices how come that the word for them doesn't read the same when held in front of one – you know, like a palindrome which I dedicated a whole rant about a while ago? It's not even an ambigram – which you might have to google – I did. I mean how pathetic is it that the mirror image for mirror is 'rorrim'? Nope it's bollox really.

Oh … and why does flipping glass have to also be so very annoying, just like sheep and fish … Eh? I mean why oh why can't these so called 'intellectual' (but clearly lazy) people who think up names for stuff actually take a little bit more time, care and consideration for the benefit of us unfortunate but hardworking simple mortals and actually invent different plural words to describe more than one of them? And the most distressing thing about this singular v plural status is (and it does stress me out – although maybe it shouldn't … or maybe I should drink less coffee) the lack of glass related consistency. I mean you have glass in one 'window' and you also have 'glass' in 10 windows. But why then is the aforementioned (a paragraph or two ago) reflective stuff's plural – mirrors' and not just 'mirror?' And even more so confusing and clearly confusingly incorrect is 'bins' … better known as spectacles. I mean these are actually called a flipping 'pair of glasses' … but there's only one … not two. And what about those world famous computer boffins who call their thingamajig Windows – how many pieces of glass make up that to be plural? Arghh!

And as for those ridiculous colourful pieces of glass in churches, you know – the stained ones – well what's that's all a-friggin'-'bout? I mean surely these cheapskate <<not a word used to describe a day's free pass at an ice rink, word – Alert>> clerics should just have paid that bit extra for clean glass instead of ridiculously coloured and lead-lined rubbish they'd bought in a local 'horse's-ass' sale? Oh – and if you're wondering what a 'horse's-ass' sale is then this was the ancient precursor to the modern day 'car-boot' sale and the same sort of thing – just less shit to trawl through with the more recent variety … literally. Although … maybe not!

So finally – and all that said, to be fair … I suppose it's actually not that difficult to tell the mood of a piece, or pieces of glass as they're really pants at hiding their emotions. I mean you can see right through them can't you. Well that is – unless they're in a bathroom (opaque) or a reflective sort (mirror) and then you're really fucked … particularly if you like a good perv … like – err … me!

And so, very finally … if it's double glazing you're faced with then just forget it … give in and walk very slowly away. I mean it's impossible to know where you are with these crafty fucker's as they're both – good and bad. Oh yeah these 'schizophrenia' dudes will really mess with your head as they've got split personalities. Yup – they're simply a real 'pane in the gl-ass'!

Holistic Hijinks Make Starfish Shun Rethinks?
Through the Ages … in Ages (Part 1 of 3 … unfortunately)

Well I suppose it all bean (I actually typed 'began' there, but hey … I like the 'baked in tomato sauce variety' so I'll leave it in for now … although if it's not there later when you read this then you'll know I had a change of mind … err?) in prehistoric times when those big footed clumsy lizards roamed the planet. Well, when I say 'roamed' I suppose I should actually rephrase that to read 'lumbered', as these leathery skinned reptilian dinosaur buggers were the size of friggin busses and heavier than … well, a herd of overweight elephants in suits of armour! As such, their movement was somewhat impaired (except for the fast ones?) and as such they were slower than bloomin' Christmas (except the fast ones) – which even on Christmas Eve still takes what seems like years to come … especially if you're a child … or an adult that hasn't grown up … like me! But of course Christmas does eventually arrive, but only after the big red-faced-bearded bugger has slid down your chimney and emptied his sack! But don't worry – I'm not going to talk about Santa or dinosaurs this time as that's for another rant … but I will, I promise (or threaten) … as I love both men in red suits and big lethargic grunting animals ... I should know as I married one (not a man in a red suit though).

So what began all those years ago? Well time did, that's what. Or more specifically the different 'ages' of time that these so-called past historical eras are now known as. And even more specifically (I've mentioned that word twice now as I'm also playing scrabble whilst typing this shite and it's worth 24 points) the 'ages of man'. Now as mentioned just before, I'm not gonna go back zillions of years to the Jurassic age of dinosaurs as a) I can't be bothered and b) man (and woman as I'm not sexist) has only been around for 200 thousand years or so ... which is way-way long after those lazy-arsed oversized lizards had decided to mysteriously disappear. Now before I go on to ponder the 'ages of man' I really must just quickly revert back to the disappearance of all of the dinosaurs ... as I actually know exactly what happened to them. Maybe.

Now – and contrary <<love this word but don't know why, word – Alert>> to popular, but misguided beliefs, dinosaurs did not become extinct on earth due to the planet being hit by a really massive 'fuck-off-sized' dirty great meteorite from outer space as originally thought. Oh no. In fact, it's now been scientifically proven (well in my head anyhow) by both Astrological (star gazers) and palaeontologist (dinosaur gazers) type boffins that these green skinned wrigglers didn't actually die out but instead simply all left earth. Basically the categorical <<not a word for the study of felines, word – Alert>> truth (well perhaps) is that they all decided to go on a mega dinosaur package-tour-pilgrimage to see and pay homage to the Great Dinosaur God – 'Uranusaurus' who lived on the planet Uranus. And as such they all (and oddly enough all at the same time) boarded a

Flintstones' style spaceship (with holes in the fuselage for feet powered take off propulsion) and headed off – rosary beads (made of boulders) in hand … err paw?

And so (and before you ask), why aren't there any dinosaurs around now? Well it's simple really. You see, although these thick-skinned dudes were huge, they had really small pea-sized brains and as such the clueless big lumps forgot to buy 'return tickets' back to earth. And therefore, they're still friggin there to this day (or the next day if your reading this tomorrow) lumbering around eating bamboo and/or each other and then dying and turning into fossils. Utter rubbish you mumble? Well no one's yet disproved this theory as fact have they … so it must be right! Or wrong! Incidentally the dinosaur God 'Uranusaurus' was well known (from ancient dinosaur cave paintings discovered in err … err … a cave) to have a very prominent backside (think Beyoncé or Kardashian style here) … and this, of course, is where we get the modern day word for bottom … 'anus'. We simply discounted the Latin bit at the end … 'cos, as I've mentioned before, Latin is complete meaningless shite.

Now at this point I'm actually very much in danger of taking about dinosaurs – so I gonna very swiftly switch back to the 'ages of man'. And so let's look at them and discover (you and me both as I'm making this rubbish up as I'm going along) why I think the whole thing is really no more than a dinosaur (worth 9 in scrabble – hence the repeated mentioning) sized pile of horse plop.

Well firstly, in a time long, long ago – it all begun with 'Apple Age', which contrary to modernistic popular belief was a long, long time ago. In fact, so long ago that God was still in short pants … although he was an old man – which was a bit of a worry. Now whilst you won't find a reference to this in any scientific books – it did actually happen, as it's mentioned in that other big, but somewhat confusingly written book – the Bible. You know the, one that's named after the French word for a baby's mess-prevention clothing protector and which is all about stuff that happened a while back ... like donkeys, heavy rain and silly star following clever guys with gifts. So Apple Age. Well this is that very ancient time when that Adam bloke (which is an anagram for 'a mad' or 'a dam' ... both of which are irrelevant here, as is anagram or 'nag a ram') thought it clever to eat an iPhone – or it could've been an iPad – but definitely an Apple ... and as such really pissed off the big guy with the white beard (in short trousers). So much so in fact, that he turned both him and his bird Eve into snakes (or was it pillars of salt ... or wine and fish?) and decided to abandon the garden-centre home he'd created for them and start again a few years later with guys who wore bear skins and liked stuff made out of rocks. Otherwise known as the 'Stone Age'. Now you might think this to be 'Class A' bullshit but don't forget – I am an expert in the Le Bib (just in case you didn't get the French reference just before there) book ... I mean not only have I read the book, but I've also seen the movie, musical, TV show ... and got the T-Shirt!

And so ... we move on to the 'Stone Age' ... Stoned freaking Age more like, as, given the rubbishy and quite pathetic evidence they left behind, they must've been permanently pissed and as high as kites. Why? Well everyone – and particularly those archaeological types (you know ... the lentil eating moustachioed weirdos – who still think it's okay to muck about with a bucket and spade even though they're adults) are always wittering on about these ancient people and the wonders they left us behind and with such vigour and passion about how 'truly amazing' they were … which when you think about it – is complete fucking bollox! I mean, all these stupid grunting assholes could conjure up was drafty houses made of stone, soil, ox-dung and straw. What's so freaking amazing about that! Bugger-fucking-all, that's what. I mean where's their castles and villas and bridges and cathedrals and stuff … nowhere, that's bleeding where. Talk about – piss poor … all these mumbling, bad teethed, non-computer literate fuckers could build was obelisks <<odd word for big standing stones, word – Alert>> and pointless stone circles and the likes. I mean look at that complete friggin bollox that is/was/should never have been … Stonehenge. Now before I launch into a tirade of abuse about this oversized 'rockery' (and I'm gonna), I think I'm confident in saying that it was built in the 'Stone Age' as they start with the same word so the clue's hopefully in the title … otherwise why not name it 'Apple Henge'? Mind you maybe it was and they did … but as it was made out of fruit it just crumbled under its own weight over the years and perished – as fruit does. Or turned into the first ever ((groan Alert)) apple crumble. Either way – they made it out of stones at some point.

So … why am I all flustered and derogatorily (I was amazed when that wasn't underlined in red as a misspelt or non-word when I type it) dismissive about Stonehenge? Well I totally fail to see what all the hype is about as in reality it's just a pile of unevenly assembled and poorly carved pebbles, plonked clumsily in a crude circle on a windswept field in Somerset … err, actually correction – Wiltshire … all English counties look the friggin same to me, well they do on a map. I mean it had no roof, no walls, no windows, no doors, no central heating, no conservatory, no bedrooms and not even a frigging bathroom … believe me … there's no place there for an ancient 'stoned-ager' to take a dump! Oh no – this pointless alleged 'National Treasure' was just a complete waste of time and effort – and if I'm totally honest – a blot on the flipping landscape. Oh, and why oh why did these ancient fuckwits have to build it so near to a very busy road that carries 1,000s of cars and lorries each day? Eh? I for one, feel so sorry for the good folk having to drive by this pointless monstrosity every day on their way to work … or to the shops … or to play bingo. It's a fucking eyesore.

"Oh but Quaggers" (I hear you protest) – "this was such an achievement bearing in mind they had no wheel or bulldozers" <<not a word for snoozing male cows, word – Alert>> "or cranes … so had to accomplish all of this by hand and with sweat, toil and muscle." Bollox – how do we know they didn't have mechanical assistance – eh? Okay no one's ever archaeologically discovered any ancient machinery … but likewise no one's ever not discovered any – have they … err? I mean, they could've all have just rusted away over 1,000s of years, couldn't they … as metal rusts! And anyhow, have you never seen the Flintstones' movie (the 1st mind – as the 2nd one was fucking shite … and not worth a wank in a sweet shop … not that I've had one – err in one), I mean they had cars and bowling alleys – so I'll bet they had mechanized building machinery. Nope … these Stone Age fuckers were simply liars and probably just buried the evidence of the availability of the heavy mechanized assistance they'd utilised so that to people in future millennia (like us now) – they'd look like friggin brain surgeons and the complete 'dogs-bollox! Stonehenge – more like Stonecringe!

So finally … didn't they have anything else better to do back in 2,600BC a part from exert loads of effort and energy building meaningless piles of junk? Clearly not … and I can only assume that both television and social media must've been really pretty shite back then. Mind you … wasn't it these fuckers who were the 1st to use a 'tablet' …?

Ostentatious Pretenders amidst Irregular Offenders!

Now why do rabbits have such great big 'fuck-off' sized ears … eh?

I mean why the fuck are they like teicecthecheightvof theirvfrihhing (I typed 'twice the size of their friggin'' there … honest) bodies and as big as satellite dishes … albeit – ridiculously pointy-shaped ones? Not that satellite dishes are pointed, of course, as they're round-shaped and as such resemble the hearing apparatus of that other ridiculously big-eared rodent – Micky 'fucking' Mouse (you might not know this little squeaky-voiced-do-gooding fucker by his middle name as most people never use it … but then I'm not most people am I … I'm me)! Now I'm not gonna rant about that daft rat-like fucker in this particular rant, as Disney truly merits a whole one to itself … so watch out in the future … or indeed past. Mind you – and that said … I sometimes just go straight ahead and spout about something planned for the future … or past – if you've already read this – which actually you can't have as I'm just deciding to 'go for it' now. Eh? Fuck me … that's wrecked my head and I'm writing this rubbish … so you've got no frigging hope.

And so Disney … see – I warned ya! Well actually … no … I'm gonna change my mind again (kinda

79

anyhow) and as such I'm not (repeat not) gonna spend a great deal of time on these daft and soppy cartoon characters in this rant and am indeed now gonna dedicate a whole rant to Disney. So therefore – and to 'keep my literary powder dry' for this future cartoon-fuelled rant … I'll just ramble on very briefly about these now … very briefly – honest).

So … Disney. Why are all their cartoon characters just named after other already named people, things or stuff? I mean where's the creativity in just copying names and applying them to some scrappy and quite frankly amateurishly scribbled drawings? "Oh that's unfair Quaggers," you're probably squawking now (particularly if you're a crow reading this), "the charters are absolute quality, and they're brilliantly drawn!" Bollox. They're not!

Well – okay … that Disney bloke could draw a bit (I'll give you that) – but the names of his main characters were really just complete poorly thought-through shite, lacking even an ounce of creativity. No … you're not having this? Well okay then … just bear (but not a Gummi one) with me and let's look at just a tiny slither of the available evidence … I mean there's:

'Pluto' – a planet (yawn)!

'Mickey' – nicked from some saint geezer in the Bible and simply shortened to mask the 'fraud'!

'Minnie' – clumsily borrowed from a ridiculously small and quite frankly stupid British car with an 'n' and an 'e' added!

'Snow White' – Yes we know it is (unless it's the stuff you've peed in and then its yellow) – but hey … wasn't her hair black?

'Lilo and Stitch' – OMG – the first fucker's a fucking inflatable bed and the latter's a stupid girlie handicraft like that festering pile of wank that is embroidery.

And finally for now … the aforementioned 'Gummi Bears' – possibly the biggest fraud of all as this is just the name for the skin that holds your teeth in place and with the name of an already known big-pawed animal added at the end in a rudimentary <<I love that not rude word, word – Alert>> and feeble attempt to hide the crime.

See what I mean … its total pants! And worse still – these clueless corporate twats could even outdo me for nonsensical tripe – and they've made zillions of squid (pounds) outta spectacularly pathetic and unimaginative cartoons and movies … yes blinking movies!

Oh and my apologies for the apparent unnecessary use of swearing back there, which I know I'm all too fond of, but it's just that these words are so very, very expressive. Personally, I absolutely love 'em … and as such have my favourites like 'cunt' and 'twat'! In fact, these are my actual favourite words of all time as they just tell it as it is. I mean – if someone calls you a 'cunt' or a 'twat' then you just instinctively know that you're probably not gonna get a Christmas card off them any year soon – so at least you know where you 'cunting' stand with them. Now as ridiculous as it might sound – I would actually encourage all people to use these kinds of informative words more often – and introduce them into their everyday vocabulary.

Now you might be cursing me here and thinking that I'm so terribly rude … potentially lewd … and most definitely uncouth <<a really old fashioned word for

rude, word – Alert>> but please don't be so harsh on me as it's not entirely my fault. Oh no … it's just the way I was reared! Steady …

Oh and at this point (or any other point if I'm totally honest) I must just go back to my earlier mention of the phrase 'change your mind', as imagine (should be … 'i-mind-gine' really … err) if you actually could … how weird would that be. I mean how would you physically do it … and even if you could – whose mind would you actually change it with or to what (if you were thinking about changing it to something other than another mind)? And if you could change it – would you be able to do it yourself like a kind of DIY brain transplant … with a steak knife, fork and dessert spoon? Ouch, that's sounds both friggin painful and messy … and hey … an awful lot of friggin cutlery washing up afterwards. Oh and bandages a plenty – plus cotton wool by the field full (does it actually grow in fields or on the back of 'cotton' sheep … who knows)? And anyhow … how on earth would you even attempt to persuade a suitable 'donor' to exchange barons (typed 'brains' … but fuck it … that 2nd glass of Merlot is just kicking in right now) with you? I mean – what if their mind was a better mind than yours … as if that was the case then you'd get no mileage whatsoever out of that proposed brain-swap – and that's a fact. Oh and that begs a question … if you were thinking of swapping minds with as total simpleton (although why I don't know) would you say to them that you'd give them a 'penny for their thoughts'? And if you did … would you get change?

And so – before I go on to rant about Rabbits (which I will … honest and cross my heart hope to die and if I lie I'll eat poo pie … eh?) I've gotta just very swiftly back up and underpin my earlier comment that 'I'm not most people!' Nope ... in fact I'm very pleased to confirm that I'm not nearly 5 billion people squished into one ... I'm just me. And as such I don't weigh like a trillion tons and I'm not the size of the moon, with a smiley round fat moony face and made of cheese ... like the moon is. Fact!

So finally ... its high time that I stopped spouting so much complete irrelevant non-related (although related or not and to what ... I don't know) shite and actually got on to the incredibly interesting topic of rabbits ... and their crazy dustbin-lid sized fucking ears?

Now aren't members of the leporidae (a shite ... err, I mean Latin word for members of the animal family that rabbits belong too) supposed to be sorta camouflage and as such deliberately hard to spot by would-be, or actual-be (err ... what?) predators? But if that's the case – then why have ears like Mr friggin Spock ... stuck atop <<a clever one word for the two words 'on top', word – Alert>> their stupid soppy fluffy furry heads? I mean surely it would be way less conspicuous, and indeed make more sense if they had those ridiculous big pointed ears plonked on the side of their faces ... you know ... like stuck to their fat furry cheeks so that only the very tiniest hairy triangular tips would stick up proud – and only a millimetre or three above their thick goofy heads. At least then it would be more conducive to the longevity of their lovable but nonetheless rodent (they are really – aren't they) lives? And they could still hear perfectly fine ... just like we can – and our ears aren't only on the side of our heads ... they're also blooming covered in a thick layer of hair! Well okay mine aren't ... covered in hair that is (as I'm as bald as a coot with alopecia), and not, not on the side of my head ... which they are! Now I've actually just checked there you know

... so I'm glad you couldn't see me! Err ... you can't can you?

Now I get it that they have to be biggish, to hear predators (didn't help Arnie's team though in the film of the same name) ... but why not wider, rather than sticky-fucky-uppy ... and hence giving the game away royally? And withbtheire (actually typed 'with their', there – but fuck it) crazy oversized ears their presence – as in 'Cooey ... I'm over here' is about as inconspicuous as a giraffe wearing a false moustache trying to get into a 'Polar Bears Only' night club! It's absolutely so bloody crackers that they're so fucking big and odd shaped ... like a boiled egg that's been stretched a tad ... err and flattened and ... covered in hair and ... err, we'll just odd-shaped!

I mean they certainly don't need to be as big as they freaking are, as as <<repeated word, but proper grammar, word – Alert>> mentioned a minute ago (or more if you paused for a pee at the end of the last paragraph) mine aren't ... and I have perfect fucking hearing! Well okay – I actually don't as the ((Cockney Rhyming Slang – Alert)) 'trouble and strife' is always 'rabbiting' (apt) on about how 'Mutton-Jeff' I am. Incidentally though – I'm not ... I've just got what most blokes in very long term relationships with ladies have evolved to suffer from – 'FTMSH' or Female to Male Selective Hearing ... also known by its Latin (yawn) name of 'iknowyourgobsmovinglove-butimnotlistening-itus!' Now I'd better just qualify and clarify matters here in case, a) my 'little swamp-donkey' (the wife) reads this and b) before any other female readers think I'm having a 'pop' at the fairer sex by being both a male chauvinist and insinuating <<great word that sounds like your consuming food whilst up to no good, word – Alert>>

that women generally spout shite. I'm not – although here's a question for you to ponder … 'If a woman says something and there's not a man around to hear her, is she still wrong?' I'm joking of course and … 'Ouch!' the blooming wife's just read that last bit and now I've got a throbbing, just-been-pulled (steady – keep it clean) flipping ear!

And going very quickly back to my own audible receptor efficiency (hearing) and notwithstanding the fact that I've just be 'earssaulted' <<new word for being clipped around the ear or having it tweaked, word – Alert>>, I actually think my hearing is pretty amazing really. I mean I could hear someone speaking in Los Angeles yesterday and it was like they were in the same freaking room as me. How brilliant was that eh? After all America is like 4,000 miles and yet I could hear every word they blooming said. Mind you, I was speaking to them on my iPhone … so I'm not sure whether that really counts. But it's still hearing across a huge distance … isn't it!

Mind you … I can see a bit too, as I was looking up in the sky the other night and astonishingly I could see the friggin moon … and that's about as far from here to the er … moon … err … or approximately 238,900 miles away – give or take the odd 10 miles or so. I tell you what … with these site (oops 'sight') and hearing qualities – maybe I should register myself as some sort of super hero, 'Quaggers Man' … he can see, he can hear … he can spout complete shite!

And so finally … as its nearly time for me to take my medication again … it's back to those crazy rabbits and their oversized ears. What's the point in it all eh … as surely they don't actually friggin well require them for their self-preservationist protection?

I mean firstly, rabbits are in reality very, very dangerous creatures indeed ... and should only ever be approached with great care and with a complete absence of frivolity. Now you're probably thinking that I'm having a right old 'senior-moment' here with my apparently absurd claim that rabbits are in fact dangerous animals – like snakes and bears ... but oh no.

I mean the word 'rabid' meaning 'violent' – was originally three words – 'rabbit is dangerous' and used to reflect the fact that in very ancient times they were seen not as fluffy, cuddly and loveable little animals that came out at Easter time ... but as vicious predators! In fact, rabbits used to (and maybe still do in the real world that exists outside of my vacuous head) go around in gangs and pick on and 'duff-up' less physical little animals ... like hamsters and squirrels! They were no doubt quite terrifying ... I mean, have you ever see the size of their teeth ... they're as big as their crazy fucking ears. Look at the most famous rabbit of all ... Bugs friggin Bunny ... he could bite through the New York telephone directory that fucker! Now over the millennia the phrase to describe rabbits' fearsome nature and reputation simply got shortened to just 'Rab' and the 1st letters of the following words – 'i' and 'd'. Hey presto 'rabid'. And that's a fact (maybe)!

Additionally, I also read (or heard – as I don't read so well) that more people are seriously injured each year by being kicked by rabbits than are hurt in flying accidents!

Or was that horses – not being involved in flying accidents though as that would be ridiculous – but inflicting harm on people by kicking them. Hmm ... I might have got that last qualification statement as to a rabbit's fearsome behaviour wrong ... but hey it's written now and anyhow it's an interesting concept ... even if complete nonsense.

And secondly (to my 'firstly' a few paragraphs ago) with their solitary diet of just carrots – (which enable you to see so well you can see in the fucking dark) isn't their eyesight supposed to be the best ever – in fact even better than that of a friggin ... err ... rabbit?

Idiosyncratic Squirrels Excogitate on Life's Perils?

Every so often (maybe once each year) you'll see it – maybe not hear it at first ... but it'll be there. Oh – fucking yeah!

You'll know it's in town as your favourite streets (if you have them ... I know I don't, but you might have ...) will be closed off to traffic to accommodate this ... and it's stupid, sweaty devotees. And it'll really inconvenience the hell out of you just so that its panting weirdo's can get their selfish and ridiculous kicks. So – what's got old Quaggers riled this week I hear you bark ... well ask ... as you're not a puppy or a tree?

Well it's simple ... the marathon. Yes, the blooming marathon or marathons.

Now what the heck's that bloody malarkey all about ... and what the fuck's the freaking point? I mean why oh why do some people feel the need to run around the streets of our towns and cities like demented zombies – with annoying and stupid (well they are to me) little numbers stuck on their chests and backs. Is that their mental age? And frankly – how freaking ridiculous is this so called 'major city event' of the year. I mean, c'mon! Now I'm no flipping brain surgeon or rocket scientist (although I do own a brain and a telescope ... although neither work, particularly the former) but even

I know that if you wanna get from A to B … or even C in a town or city you just need to hop into any one of the countless and readily available passing cabs – or indeed any mode of public transport that's always available. There is no need whatso-fucking-ever to dick about in a pair of running shoes and go off on a 26-mile jog. I mean it's the 21st century for Christ's sake and we've got friggin cars, busses and trains. There's no blinking need to run anymore – for fuxsake … when will these 'headband' wearing loonies wake up and smell the coffee? And talking of getting from A to B (and/or C) why oh why do they have to run up and down and around and about the streets like 'sense of directionless' crazy hamsters … and for 26 freaking miles? 26 miles, I'll bet their C to B or B to A desired destinations are only a frigging couple of hundred yards away. Are they barnstormingly <<unusual and long lost origins for a word meaning 'bonkers', word – Alert>> crackers and possessing absolutely no realization of distance? Or have they just got way too much time on their hands as to enable them to fanny around on the roads and streets of our towns and cities? Who freaking knows!

And as for those complete twonks that dress up in stupid 'fancy (it's not, believe me … it's naff) dress' … well they just really do my freaking head in like crazy! I mean, and call me old fashioned (actually no – just call me Gaz) but if they wanna prance about in public in their 'weekend' fetish clothes then why don't they just remain within the confines of their own houses … and 'mince' around? Now I don't know about you, but I get absolutely no pleasure whatsoever from seeing panting people jogging about on our streets dressed as giant frogs, hippos … or scantily clad burlesque dancers. Well okay, may be the latter makes me tingle a little … but hey, that's private … so just forget I ever penned that last bit will ya. Thanks. (;0).

Anyhow …

And as for those so-called 'do-gooders' who run because they are raising money – well that just really 'grips-my-shit' (not literally … but you know)! It even pisses me off more than my other pet hates <<silly, as I actually love pets, phrase – Alert>>, which are of course … Rallying (pretentious fast car bollox), cyclists (get a bike with a fucking engine and stop riding in pairs you lycra clad knob-ends) and horse riders (oh my god … it's a public road you're on … not a fucking bridle path you selfish jodhpur wearing freaks). Now, boy … do these guys really piss on my chips – majorly or what … although you're probably gathering that by now)! (;0) Oh, and quickly 'trotting' (see what I've done there?) back to horses, well I'm gonna dedicate a whole rant to these equestrian (<<stupid 'horsey' word for horse, word – Alert>> nuisances one day very soon. No, really.

So 'raising frigging money' I mean why oh why … and what's the fucking point?

I mean what's wrong with money at normal height … why do these 'goody-freaking-two-shoes' types feel that there is a need to elevate it to a greater height … or have I just got the wrong end of the stick again. Mind you, is there correct end of a stick? Err … moving on …

So running around streets … why do it? I mean what is the point of running around like a demented twat (and I make no apologies for using that word … and anyhow – it's typed now)? It's not as if they're gonna get any remuneration <<big word for wages – Alert>> for there ('their' … even) efforts! Oh, and if it's to keep fit then that's a complete and total waste of time that is, as it's a scientifically proven fact that the most effective way to keep fit is simply to eat less pies. Honest!

Oh, and hey <<<Breaking News>>> I've got news for these feckless running types … who love boasting that they've completed a 'half marathon'. Do what? Now although I bloody hate marathons (from the Ancient Greek word 'marathon' – meaning sweating whilst dicking about), what even gnaws at my bits more is those useless buggers who run only half the distance. I mean what's the freaking point of that – it's like doing half a job.

Imagine a 100 meters' sprinter like that Usain Bolt – 'bolting' off (so that's where he got his silly surname from … probably christened plain old 'Usain Smith') and running faster than 'hot shit off a shovel' … and then pulling up after just 50 meters. Half a job.

Or imagine going for a 'Donald Trump' (a dump) or 'Tom-Tit' (a shit) and after you'd opened the bomb doors and released the vegetable-matter-fused ordnance … you just then got up and sauntered <<love that sexy sounding … but not really meaning sexy, word – Alert>> off without first having wiped your 'chocolate starfish' or 'rusty sheriff's badge' with bum wad? Now that would be half a job … well a full job but with only half the job done … err?

So what news have I got for these half a job and frankly quite pathetic 'half-marathoneers' <<made up word … but, hey … let's run with it, word – Alert>>? Well it's this:

A marathon – and for the simple but stupid reason that Ancient Greeks couldn't count as the solar powered calculator hadn't then been invented (which is odd as they had an abundance <<not a rhythmic movement for

cakes, word – Alert>> of sun) is actually a little bit over 26 miles. Indeed, it's actually 26 miles and 385 yards.

Now the reason for this randomly odd race length was solely down to the fact that there was actually a 'Feta cheese and ouzo' fast food outlet just (but exactly to the inch) 385 yards from the finishing line of the 1st ever marathon race in Athens … in AD … something or other.

And so … when the first ever marathoneer 'Pheidippides' <<really crazy name but it actually was his, word – Alert>> completed the race after running off from the Battle of Marathon (he needed to get home from the scene of the fighting as he'd remembered he left the kettle on), he'd worked up such an appetite and thirst that when he spotted saw the aforementioned fast food eatery – he simply carried on running. The rest is history – or at worst … his-story!

Now before you have me carted off by the men in white coats to a nice padded cell with pictures of disenfranchised teapots suspended from papier-mâché walls, this is now a proven scientific and an archaeological fact. Indeed, as the remains of this establishment were unearthed in the 1920s … when they found an old stone and iron grilled oven, lots of clay plates and a sign made out of petrified wood (it wasn't scared though) which still (albeit faintly) – bore the name 'Alex-Nando's-the Grate'. No really!

So you'll now no doubt (especially if you're 'Gwen Stefani') be screaming – "What's the frigging news you got then for people who've run half marathons?" Well it's simply this … they haven't! Now they might've run hundreds of silly 'half-a-job' races … but the reality is that they've never actually completed one. I shit you not.

I'm talking tosh you think? Well no, because each time they've only run 13 miles – which even I know (and I make pig-shit look like a college graduate) is not half of 26 miles and 385 yards. To complete a proper 'half marathon – they would've needed to have actually ran 13 miles and (hang on a mo' whilst I get my solar powered calculator and go outside) ... 192.5 yards. So there ... stupid cheating fraudulent buggers!

Mind you – if I subsequently find out that they do actually run 13 miles and 192.5 yards – then please just ignore the last couple of paragraphs ... and take a nap!

So ... all this running around our towns and cities is just a complete load of nonsense and a massive waste of taxpayers' money ... I'll wager! Well I would if I had any wages left, which I haven't as they'd all been spent on taxes funding meaningless and daft running races.

Anyhow ... all this talk of running around is making me really tired ... so I think I'll actually go and run. Now before you think I'm a contradictory buffoon ... or 'fuckwit' <<a non-dictionary ... but should be, word – Alert>> ... I'm actually not about to put on a pair of shorts, a vest and training shoes ... or get dressed up as a hippo (well not just yet). Nope ... I'm actually about to go and run ... a bath!

Mind you, if I did physically run a bath – I win easily ... no sweat. I mean – although some baths have 4 feet (the ones that just sit flat to the floor or are sunken into it if you're posh – have none), I still reckon they'd be as slow as freaking Christmas in a running race ... and could be easily 'outrun' by an overweight tortoise with ingrowing toenails! Or me!

So that's about it for this week ... but hey – before I go and wallow and soak ... I can't leave you without a quick swerve back to 'training shoes'. Why are they called that? I mean what are they still training for ... why aren't they fully trained when you buy them? No really. It's like paying top dollar for a puppy that hasn't stopped shitting in the house – you wouldn't would you – you'd buy a 'trained' one ... not one in training! It's a friggin joke to call then training shoes ... I call my 'Trained Shoes' ... as they fit ... and don't shit! And as for those crazy yanks calling them 'sneakers' ... WTF is all that about. I mean do they really use them to creep up on people ... and if so why? Are they all peeping Toms?

Nope ... the correct name is a pair of 'Trained Shoes'.

Incommodious Twine Amplifies Spice Museum's Wine!

Imagine being a bird. I mean how absolutely fooking depressing must that be – eh? Now before you chastise <<infrequently used word, word – Alert>> me and accuse me of being derogatory to the fairer sex … I'm not actually talking about some really 'fit' and 'tasty' lady. Oh no. Remarkably (as ladies are indeed a favourite subject of mine … along with cheese and Lego … err), I'm actually talking about our feathered friends. That said, I have actually imagined being a bird on numerous occasions … a lady bird, mind … and not a feathered type – as feathers would no doubt tickle my bits (and I prefer to do that myself with my hands) … err, maybe I shouldn't have typed that! Oh and not the insect version of a lady bird either … as that would be ridiculous – and anyhow … I don't like sitting on plants wearing a black and red spotted coat! Indeed … being a lady often crosses my mind and – 'in fact' <<two words that should be one word, words – Alert>>

Oh … so cheese and Lego. Well I love cheese and the stronger the better – mature (like me) Cheddar … but I'll come back to cheese another day as I've (and probably not a surprise) got a lot to say about deliberately curdled cow's milk … or goat's … or both if it's from a crossbred cow and goat … a 'coat'.

So that leaves Lego. Well I absolutely love these multi coloured plastic bricks. Now whilst it's globally famous – most people don't actually know where it got its name from. Well 230 years ago (or maybe a lot more recently) a middle aged man called 'Ivor Plastikken Brikken' <<common Danish surname alert … err, maybe>> who lived in Copenhagen in Denmark – invented a new (well it would have to be if he'd invented it) toy. Out of a simple brick. Bricks were and still are the national export of Denmark – which was originally called Denbrik … (hmm the bullshit meter is going off the scale this time). Anyway – he tried this new brick themed toy out on his children and found that he couldn't get it back off them … they just wouldn't let-go … or 'Lego'. And of course, as everyone knows, 'Lego' is the Danish word for 'stuck to hand' (well it might be)! Hence and hey presto … Lego!

Anyhow, and back to talking about our feathered friends … why are they actually called that. I mean it's not like they're that flipping friendly (like a dog) and how do we know that they actually even like us – never mind actually being our friends. Oh – and what the fuck's 'ornithology' all about. Bird watching … how crazy is that … and a bit weird if you ask me (which you haven't – but I'll answer anyway)! I mean sitting quietly and patiently, hiding in a bush with a pair of binoculars (I'll come back to those in a mo') and a flask of coffee and some sandwiches (cucumber and watercress I'll bet), watching little feathered animals for hours on end. How terribly sad and worrying – if I'm honest – is it that some 'so-called' grown-ups get their kicks spying on geese and ducks and the likes, going about their everyday business … like eating, going to the toilet, combing their hair and bonking! No bloody wonder they call it 'ornithology' – some big clever word to disguise or mask the fact that they're practitioners of a quite frankly ridiculous and somewhat sleazy hobby! Why can't they just admit that they're weirdoes and call it 'featherorgasminology'! They'd be better using their spare time to watch the other type of blooming birds – at least that's normal and not sleazy …!

Now, I'm not one to veer off the subject, but I feel a very quick digression <<clever word, word – Alert>> … is warranted here. A 'pair' of binoculars? Now whilst undoubtedly a very clever invention … there is only one of them … not two … so why call them a blooming 'pair'? I once bought a 'pair' of binoculars and as soon as I'd opened the box – I took them back to the shop and angrily demanded my money back on discovering that I only had one … I remember that I clearly asked the shop assistant for a 'pair' of binoculars!

So … and hang about … in mentioning 'feathered' friends … I've just remembered another thing that makes that saying ridiculous. Not all birds actually have feathers. No. I mean first of all there's an American bald eagle – so no hair … err feathers (hence its name). They weren't always a bald species of bird though – oh no … there's a good story as to how that happened and as it's not your lucky day – I'm gonna 'spill'! Yeah it's an actual fact (well maybe) that the American 'bald' eagle was originally – back at the dawn of time – very, very feathery indeed! Yep they were originally called 'hairy eagles' – but alas they were actually very afraid of both heights and flying … so over the millennia – their feathers fell out due to worry and stress! And hence they've evolved to be bald today (really)! Oh – and then there's penguins – who aren't really birds at all … they're chocolate biscuits made especially for people with stutters!

So ... by now, you've probably given up the will to live or wondering when is he gonna tell us why our feathered friends – the birds ... are so unfortunate.

Well – it's just that every time you walk past them- they have to fuck – (okay fly) off ... I've got Tourette's you know. Well I'm bastard-bum-fucking-cock-tits wank ... convinced I have. Anyway, these poor birds are just sitting (or shitting – if they do that sitting down) ... minding their own birdie business – when all of a sudden – you walk past and up and away they have to go. It's like they get a sudden impulse to just have to 'do one'. They must be on blooming pins – not ever being able to rest ... in case someone wanders by. Of course, this is a really distressing and somewhat tiresome and painful experience for caged birds – as every time they fly off when you walk past – 'bang' – they hit their heads on the roof of the flipping cage! I really think that there should be a law that makes it compulsory for people who own caged birds to have to buy little crash helmets for them ... or fit a padded roof to their cages – made out of soft foam rubber ... coloured blue to look like the sky!

And what about bird food. Their diet is made up entirely out of small pieces of bread – and we're not talking croutons here – and worms ... oh and with the odd wild berry thrown in for an occasional dessert. How incredibly boring must that be – and bad for your health as well – as bread is a carb and worms give you ... err ... worms! I'll bet that birds must have a real poor diet ... except for the berries ... but even most of those are poisonous ... and at best will give them the 'squits'. I bet there must be bird hospitals full of err ... birds – suffering from years of neglecting their bird bodies by consuming unhealthy food. No blooming wonder that so called 'bird-flu' was so popular a few years ago ...

probably caused by unhealthy birds with rubbishy diets … farting and spreading bottom vapour germs amongst themselves. Mind you – do birds really get the Flu – and if so, what are the symptoms and how can you tell. I mean they're just birds – you can't take their temperature by sticking a thermometer up their bums or feel their foreheads for a fever … as they're covered in blooming feathers. And anyhow – what would you give them if they had the flu … (sorry about this) … parrotcetemol?

So I really think that we should show our feathered friends some real love and kindness and in future put out nice food for them … like pizza and jam sponge cake … and perhaps cream of tomato soup … although how good they'd be at holding a spoon is anyone's guess!

So … there you have it … birds really, really have a miserable time of it and are so very unlucky to be born birds.

Oh … but hang about one god dang minute … I suppose they can fly – which admittedly … is pretty incredibly awesome. So they're actually very lucky indeed … hmm, what a waste of words this nonsense has been then! Oops … I'd better fly … which of course I can't!

Krakatoa Roulette's Bake Poltergeist Baguettes?

Hadrian's Wall, the Colosseum, Julius Caesar, Pompeii, gladiators, togas and pizza. Yes … the theme of this week's rubbish is – Romans! Or put another way – this week's theme is 'rubbish Romans' … as let's face it – they were. Conquered the world … well fuck knows how that happened. I mean, our ancient forefathers (and foremothers … if I'm not being sexist) must've been having a freaking afternoon nap when those daft skirt-wearing-feather-helmet-headed-Latin-speaking dipsticks were running around taking over the half the known world! Oh, and as for what progress they made in the unknown bit of the world … god only knows – and even he doesn't. Eh?

So … back to those stupid (and no, this isn't being unfair) bloody Romans. I mean let's look at the evidence to see precisely (maybe) how rubbishy they actually were … it's there for all to see – honest.

I mean who the fucjk <<Serbian for the word 'fuck' or just big fingered typing, word – Alert>> would be in awe – let alone, be fearful of a bunch of Italian speaking geezers dressed in skirts and sandals. Eh? No one – that's who.

And as for the things I mentioned at the outset of this nonsense – well, Hadrian's Wall (he didn't build it) and whoever did – why? I mean who would really want to go to all that trouble to build an oversized garden wall (albeit a fooking long one) up in the wilds of freaking Scotland … where at the time … all the locals were wild-foaming-at-the-mouth-savage-like simpletons, wearing even more dubious skirts with silly chequered patterns on. Mind you, nothing's really changed much on that score has it … I mean I went to Scotland recently and it was closed! Mind you – I suppose you shouldn't expect too much from a country that's staple diet consists of sheep's bladders filled with offal (it tastes absolutely shit … I'll bet, as I've not actually tasted it) and lumpy porridge (just white sloppy goo) with salt. They even do rude 'sexy' things with cut-down tree trunks … like what us normal 'non-ginger haired' folk do with pancakes – but with trees instead of … err pancakes? Anyway back to Romans …

Then there's the Colosseum. Nothing much to be in awe of here as it was just a sort of sports stadium made out of no doubt poor grade concrete – and without a freaking roof. Yeah – I've seen pics of it and it's true … as although they could invent all sorts of supposedly useful stuff … they didn't even have the brains to stop the spectators getting freaking wet whenever their Gods decided to take a leak on them!

As for Julius Caesar … well, simply a guy with a girl's name, donning a silly floral headband – who pretended to be important but really only invented a freaking salad … and a rubbish one at that as no boiled eggs or beetroot – which are of course the corner stone of any salad worth it's … err salt?

Then there's Pompeii … nothing much to write about here as just a town populated by heavy smokers with clearly no ashtrays and a crappy fire department. Hmm …?

Oh – and gladiators. Well – okay, it might've been a great film but were there really people who talked Australian and who were named after birds living in ancient in Rome mucking about with swords and tridents <<meaning 3, word – Alert>>? I think not … how freaking absurd.

And as for their habit of wearing the 'off battlefield' casual attire … the 'toga' – how ridiculous was that. I mean how the feck could anyone afford a bunch of guys any credibility whatsoever if they swanned about 'off-piste' <<love that phrase although I don't ski, word – Alert>> … in a glorified white sheet? Ridiculous!

Then there's the exceedingly overrated pizza. I mean this Roman flat bread invention with random left over stuff tossed on top of it is really not worthy of having such global acclaim is it. And hey … was it really that necessary to have a gradually toppling over building named after it (you might have to think about that one … as I might be talking complete shite)!

And finally – what about freaking 'Roman numerals' … what the fucks all that blooming malarkey all about. Eh? Letters as flipping numbers … how ridiculous is that.

Well fortunately for you – I've rambled on enough this time … but be warned – I'll come back to this topic again in a future rant.

Nope … I think the historians must have got things totally 'ass-about-face' and the truth was that the Romans didn't fight their way across half the known world with ruthlessness and untold bravery. No … all they did was to simply show up … pull a few clever (but at the time – jaw dropping cutting edge) inventions out of their bags – like underfloor heating, baths and grapes … and hey presto … everyone wants a piece of their ass … and they're everyone's best friends all of a sudden.

So – that's enough about our ancient skirt wearing Italian cousins for now – as I'm going to go and slip into my toga (not 'tiger' mind … as that'd be ridiculous and frankly quite dangerous … unless it was stunned) and have a pizza.

Reptilian Anchovies Clone Hard to Please Hercules?

Now I don't go to church as much as I should I suppose ... but hey no one's perfect – as no one's no one and therefore no one can be perfect as they're no one ... err? Anyhow as for going to church ... well I'm a 'for special occasions only' attendee – you know ... hatches, matches and dispatches. But that said I do kinda know what goes on in these buildings on non-special occasions – it's praying and singing ... or is it the other way around? That is what they do isn't it? Anyway – I was there (at church) the other weekend for a wedding ... or was it a funeral (I forget now) ... and the guy standing at the front of the congregation <<unnecessary (as is that one) longish word for a gathering of people, word – Alert>> in a dress type thing, repeated a phrase a couple of times that really set my 5 amp brain a thinking.

That thought was simply this ... do they really know how to pray?

I mean do they? And do they <<not a repeated question but actually two – using the same words, words – Alert>> actually do it? And if so – how the freaking hell do they achieve it ... eh? I mean, can they kneel by their beds and bow their heads? And do they even have beds? Well in a veritable sea of questions – I'll give you one quick answer before you suffer a panic attack of severe 'questionosis' <<just made up word for the phobia of being presented with lots of statements with question marks at the end, word – Alert>>. And so yes … they actually do have beds … err, what was the question again?

So … what the freak's this complete loon thinking of and going on about this time you fear. We'll … be afraid, very afraid … and more so than a fish suffering from chronic aquaphobia … as this one registers an 8.4 on the 'Shitcer scale' (a recently made up scale, but one that is used to accurately measure the magnitude of complete bullshit). Well it's simple. Its vegetables, or to be precise … vegetables and religion … or put even more precisely … are vegetables religious?

Now – scoff thee not … oh no. Remember that vicar bloke or was he a priest or just a random guy in a long dress at the church that I mentioned a while back. Well he said on at least 2 occasions (or was it 15) the following phrase – 'lettuce pray'. No really! Now although I'm probably a bit 'Mutton Geoff' these days (as age creeps up on me like a clumsy samurai with an ill-fitting wooden leg) … I definitely heard him utter the words 'lettuce pray'. So do they? And even more moorland (typed 'important' there … but?), why mention this in the house of God and in apparent random isolation?

I mean what gives edible plant thingy things the right to have their religious worshipping habits mentioned in our churches? Why are they so flipping important? They don't even go to church very often – less than me in fact – as they only ever turn up once a frigging year for a harvest festival! And only then so they can sit on tables right up at the front looking all smug as the centre of attention and be blessed and lauded over by the bloke in the dress.

And why lettuces? I mean of all the vegetables out there … this bugger is way, way, way the dullest of them all. I mean it sits around half in-half out of the ground and wearing nothing but the totally common and standard stereotypical <<love that word but don't know why, word – Alert>> boring vegetable colour – green! And all it tastes of is blinking water (not water that winks at ya BTW – as water don't do that and anyhow doesn't have eye … so I should've said – just water) which makes it the most totally pointless veg there has ever been. Only people on diets and rabbits eat this tasteless trash so why oh why religious sorts see the need to have to even have to remind us of their worshiping habits is just so truly beyond me. Oh, and why not the potato? I mean surely if there is such an ecclesiastical <<big word for religion, word – Alert>> need or requirement for referring to the fact that random stuff believes in God, then surely the potato should out-rank the flipping lettuce. I mean, at least potatoes have got skin and eyes … and make great fries … which can't be made out of, yes you've guessed … a stupid lettuce! Mind you – corn has ears … but hey I digress as that's not a vegetable is it – it's a cereal … or if you eat it and it repeats on you then it's a serial. Hmm …

Mind you – and all that said … a lettuce did manage to sink the Titanic … so maybe they're … err I don't actually know how to finish this sentence … so I won't?

But anyhow – and moving swiftly on – why be so specific to this particular veg or vegetables in general. I mean why not just say 'people pray', or if they wanted to widen the appeal and be more politically correct – then why not 'animals pray' as this would be factually correct as people are animals and it's not stretching it too ridiculously far too perhaps suggest that some types of 'non-human' animals do indeed pray. You know, say to a higher almighty being … err like a Cat God. I mean the Egyptians worshipped our feline friends didn't they. And beatles, but hey … not the silly mop-haired '60s pop group ones – as although the 1960s were hundreds of years ago … the Scouse warblers didn't actually burst onto the scene with their daft lyrics until long after the triangular loving Nile dwellers had done one … and gone and hidden somewhere. Maybe they went into permanent hibernation as they were in de-Nile about something. Maybe the futility of idolizing cats … who know, who cares? Oh and very quickly back to the Beatles (they weren't BTW – they were people – so stupid name as well) as I'm meant to be ranting about religious vegetables. Well, you might think I was being a tad unfair to call their lyrics 'daft' … but they were! I mean, in not one of their 'so called' hits is there any reference whatsoever to the internet or Wi-Fi, or even Bluetooth <<odd word that has nothing to do with rubbish dentists, word – Alert>>. Nope, not one. There's not even any mention of iPhones or mobile phones in general … WTF? These 'insect-obsessed' fools were clueless and in all honesty they at best displayed complete, unprofessional naivety or at worst – just sheer intellectual ignorance. The blooming Beatles … bollox – the 'dinosaurs' would've been more friggin apt!

Now you'll be relieved to hear that we're nearly there – so I'll quickly go back to the subject matter (well part of it) as I feel I really have to reiterate that vegetables are just that … vegetables. They're nothing special. Now I'm not being unfair … it's just that they don't even serve a purpose apart from to blooming eat! Well okay – some like … err … err … pumpkins can be used for fashioning crude lamps out, carrots make excellent noses for snowmen and of course onions can (with the aid of a piece of string) be fashioned into necklaces for bicycle loving French men in stupid hats. Oh and let's not forget cucumbers which can be used for a bit of fun if you're on your own and in need of some naughty relief – or if you're really up for it then melons can serve the same purpose!

Oh – one more very quick thing – that one question that I did actually answer earlier on in this rant, you know … the one … that vegetables do sleep in beds. Now whether they use pillows made out of gathered up soil, or have nightmares … we'll probably never know … but like flowers, vegetables do in fact grow in beds! Or is that patches?

ABOUT THAT YEAH:

Time for some even lighter relief ...

A bloke with Tourette's goes into the library and says, "Hey, ASSHOLE, have you got the latest book on Tourette's?"

The librarian says, "Fuck off, you cunt."

The bloke says, "Yep, that's the one."

I'm beginning to think that the female body was designed by the local council.

I mean ... who else would put a play area next to a shit house?

News just in ...

The Irish have solved their own fuel problems.

They imported 50 million tonnes of sand from the Arabs and they're going to drill for their own oil ...!

Just bought the wife a Pug dog.

Despite the squashed nose, bulging eyes, rolls of fat and being ugly as fuck, the dog seems to like her …

A man noticed two dads arguing on the side of a football field over whose son had the better ball control. He interrupted, and said, "Calm down, lads. They're both awful."

Angered, they yelled, "And how would you fucking know?"

He replied, "I'm their priest."

Rihanna, Usher and Bieber are walking over a bridge.

Rihanna trips and gets her head stuck between the railings.

Without a sideways glance, Usher pulls aside her G-String and fucks her senseless.

He stands back and tells Justin, "Your turn"!

Justin burst out into tears. "What's wrong?" asks Usher …

Bieber replies … "It might hurt when I stick my head between the railings!"

I was starting my new job at the chemist this morning when some bloke walked in.

"I've got a blocked nose, a sore throat and my head feels like it's going to fucking explode," he said. "Have you got anything?"

I said, "No mate, I feel fucking fine."

I made a real effort when I went out the other night, and I ended up pulling.

Unfortunately, it was my own fucking cock as usual!

My wife just texted me; 'If you know what's fucking good for you, you'll get yourself home right fucking now!'

Awesome. No time to finish my pint, looks like I'm on for a blow job!

"Doctor. My husband prefers to masturbate rather than have sex with me, can you suggest anything? "

"Have you tried wearing anything to make sex more appealing to him?" said the doctor.

"Yes doctor: sexy underwear, stockings, boots, garters, I've tried the lot."

"No," said the doctor "… I meant like a brown paper bag, or something. "

Q. What's a priest and a pint of Guinness got in common?

A. A black coat, white collar and you've got to watch your arse if you get a dodgy one!

Paddy, the Irish boyfriend of the woman whose head was found on Arbroath beach was asked to identify her.

A detective held up the head to which Paddy said …

"I don't think that's her … she wasn't that tall!"

Paul McCartney's ex – Heather Mills' new boyfriend has bought her a plane for her birthday.

But she'll still use Veet on the other leg!

The wife bought some crotchless knickers …

"What do you think?" she winked, bending over.

"Nice," I replied. "It reminds me of the time I opened up a bin bag round the back of the abattoir."

I just told my wife that I'm heading down the pub and she threw her cooking all over the floor.

Silly fucking cow. Now she's got to clean that up …

And on our wedding anniversary of all days!

I'm not saying my wife has a hairy fanny … but the first time I saw her naked I thought she was wearing a fucking sporran!

A girl is about to jump off a bridge when a truck driver comes past and says, "What ya doing?"

She replies, "I'm committing suicide."

The driver then says, "Before you jump, can you gimme a BJ?"

The girl nods and does her thing.

Afterwards the driver says, "Wow you've got a real talent there. Why are you committing suicide?"

"Because my parents don't like me dressing up as a girl!"

A man walks into confessional, and says to the priest, "Bless me, father, for have sinned … I had sex with seven different women last night."

The priest is silent for a moment – then says, "Go home, and cut seven lemons in half, squeeze the juice into a glass, and drink it down in one gulp."

"And I'll be forgiven?" asks the man.

"No," replies the priest, "but it will wipe that fuckin' smirk of your face!"

While strolling round the harbour this morning about 11 a.m. I noticed a terrorist slip from the quayside and fall into the water.

He was struggling to stay afloat because of all the explosives he was carrying. If he didn't get help he'd surely drown.

Being a responsible citizen, and abiding by the law of the land that requires you to help those in distress, I informed the police, the coastguard, the immigration office and even the fire dept.

It is now 4 p.m., he has drowned, and none of the authorities has yet responded.

… I'm starting to think I wasted four fucking stamps!

Today I got the wife one of those handy little safety devices specifically designed to help women drivers avoid accidents.

A fucking bus pass!

A woman places an ad in the local newspaper.

'Looking for a man with three qualifications:

1) He won't beat me up,

2) He won't run away from me, and

3) Is great in bed.'

Two days later her doorbell rings.

"Hi, I'm Tim. I have no arms so I won't beat you, and no legs so I won't run away."

"Okay – so what makes you think you're great in bed?" the woman retorts.

Tim replies, "I rang the fucking doorbell, didn't I?"

I was in McDonald's today and this really fit young bird took my order.

"I can make it large for you for an extra 50p," she said sweetly.

"You already fucking well have, love," I replied, "so how about a wank for a £1?"

I was lying on the doctor's examination table today when she asked, "How is your libido?"

"My what?" I replied.

"Libido," she said. "Do you feel like having sex?"

"Okay," I replied, "but we'll have to be quick, my wife is waiting in the fucking car."

A woman in India has given birth to a 23lb baby boy.

Doctors say they expect the baby to be walking 6 months before his mum!

I took the wife to a disco at the weekend. There was a guy on the dancefloor giving it large; breakdancing, moonwalking, backflips … the works! My wife turned to me and said, "See that guy. 25 years ago we were engaged to get married but I broke it off!"

I said to her … "Looks like he's still fucking celebrating!"

My wife's sister sat on my glasses and broke them earlier. I was really pissed off.

Then I thought … 'To be fair, it was my fucking fault for leaving them on!'

My mate has just been thrown off the medical register for having sex with a patient,

Shame … he was a bloody good vet!

I asked my wife what she wanted for her birthday.

"Something that buzzes and is guaranteed to drive me fucking crazy," she replied.

So I bought her a pet mosquito.

My girlfriend told me that she thinks I'm crap in bed.

I said, "Well, when we had sex last night I didn't hear you fuckin' moaning!"

The wife was looking at google on her iPad the other day and she said to me …

"Did you know that a bull fucks up to 1,000 times a year why … can't you do that?"

I replied: "Ask the blooming bull if he fucks the same miserable cow every night!"

The recession has hit my wife so hard she's started fucking sleeping with me again as she can't afford batteries …

What's a definition of disappointment?

Running into a wall with an erection and breaking your nose!

Does anyone know where those sumo guys get their outfits from?

I'm thinking about getting the wife a thong for her birthday.

My dwarf girlfriend went to work this morning really annoyed with me, because I've been taking the piss out of her size.

So I'm going all out to make it up to her tonight.

I've got a good bottle of wine in and bought her the latest DVD box set of her favourite romantic drama programme.

When she gets in from work I'm going to order her favourite takeaway for her dinner … then go upstairs and run her a nice hot sink.

Today, my mate was doing a crossword and asked me if I knew the biological word for a swollen vagina.

I thought … 'Thick twat!'

I'm not saying my new girlfriend's a slut … but, she's been banged more times than a snooze button on a Monday morning!

My dad worked on the roads for twenty years before he got fired for stealing! At first I didn't believe it … but when I got home all the signs were there.

I asked my neighbour if it has been hard since him and his wife separated.

He said, "Yes … quite a few times!"

If I had a pound for every time my wife wasted money on a ridiculous impulse buy, I'd have enough cash to complete the restoration of the 17th century musket I won on eBay.

The wife was having a go at me:

"Life's just one big bloody joke to you, isn't it?"

"I don't know what you mean. Sit down luv, and let's talk about it."

That's when I pulled her fucking chair away!

I can hear the lesbian couple next door to me having sex every fucking night.

It's not fucking easy mind, but if I turn the TV off and unplug the fridge, I can just about hear them.

I've only got a 4″ cock.

Mind you I'll bet some women don't like it that thick!

Scientists have just announced that you are more likely to die of what your grandad died of, rather than your father as they first thought.

For fuck's sake … if anyone sees any German snipers knocking about please let me know!

I'm sure my mate Dave is having an affair with my wife.

He's been a fucking miserable bastard lately!

Some bloke walked up to the counter and said, "Burger and chips, please."

"Certainly, Sir," I replied. "Are you eating in or taking out?"

"Fuck off you bastard," he snapped, before walking off with his food.

I love working in the prison canteen.

My wife told me I had a small penis, so I said that it was big enough to blooming well hurt her.

"There isn't a woman in the world that would be hurt by that tiny fucking thing!" she scowled.

I then showed her a video of me shagging her sister. "I've never been so hurt in all my life," she screamed.

"Argument fucking won," I replied.

I entered a wanking contest with some of the other bus drivers at work today.

Nothing happened for about fifteen minutes …

… then three of us came at once.

Trying to close your internet porn window when you hear the wife coming is like trying to get your keys in the door when you're dying for a piss!

I phoned my girlfriend, and said, "I was thinking … dinner at my place tonight, think you can make it?"

She said, "I'll be there at seven, babe."

I replied, "Make it five, the dinner won't fucking prepare itself."

Went out last night, got pissed out of my mind.

I woke up this morning next to this ugly minging sweaty bird, who was snoring, grunting and farting.

I thought, 'Thank fuck for that, at least I made it home safe…!'

My wife was putting sun cream on.

"Do you mind doing my back?" she asked.

"Let's pretend I'm your butler," I winked. "My name's Dawes."

"Ok!" she giggled. "Would you mind doing my back, Dawes?"

And that was all the fucking invitation I needed …!

I was working in the bar when some hot bird started flirting with me.

She asked, "What time do you get off?"

"I'm not sure," I replied. "I don't really schedule my wanks!"

My boss said to me, "Why do you come out in a rash every time I give you your wages?"

I said, "It's because I'm allergic to fucking peanuts."

A Welsh bloke, fuckin his Mrs says, "Do you fancy a bit of anal?"

She snapped back, saying, "No bloody way ... my friend Shirley told me that really hurts ..."

Taffy turned to her and said, "It'll be ok love, I will do you up the arse, and if it starts to hurt ... just yell out the safety word, and I'll stop."

"Alright ..." she said. "What's the safety word?"

Taffy says ... "Llanfaerpullgwyngythgorgerychwyndrobwthllandysiliogogogoch!"

I was cuddling with my girlfriend under the blanket on a cold winter night.

"My arse is freezing," she whinged.

"Let me check," I replied. "Holy shit, it's like Siberia!"

"It's that cold?" she chuckled.

I said, "No, it's fuckin huge."

On my first day in prison, my cellmate said to me, "If you ever come close to me, I'll fucking skin you. When we're sleeping, you don't fucking touch me. You hear me? Don't ever talk to me, either."

'Fucking great,' I thought '… first day in here and I'm already married!'

I once went for a job as a blacksmith.

The bloke asked me if I'd ever shoed a horse.

I said, "No … but I once told a donkey to fuck-off!"

Parsimonious Cuddles Augment Stoic Rebuttals?

Okay, so it doesn't quite rhyme. But hey … if you look closely … or actually just glance (as it's not worth a more detailed observation) at the 'Pantsrantians' <<made up word meaning nonsensical ramblings, word – Alert>> Rule Book – you'll see that it doesn't actually say anywhere that the 'subject headers' have to rhyme.

Okay, so I'll level with you … it doesn't say it anywhere because it literally doesn't say anything anywhere – as there isn't actually a Pantsrantians' rule book … and even if there was there wouldn't be. Eh? I mean how would it be possible to have in place, sitting quietly on the shelf (doing its nails or hair), a rule book about a subject or thing that had only just been invebtebed (typed 'invented' there?) a few lines back? Frankly (back to that in a mo') it would be ridiculously impossible or improbable (never understood the difference there – and back to that as well in a mo-mo … groan) to have a rule book with rules made up, written and printed in a matter of seconds – and by whom (which is a posher way of saying 'who'). Nope it couldn't happen – well unless you had a time machine and could make some complete shite up (err … like I just have) and then simply go back in time (or would it be forward?) and wrote the rules for it. Now I ain't got a time machine ... well okay, I've got a watch, oh and there are clocks on the walls ... you know, 'wall clocks'. But hey ... all they do is tell the flipping time – which thinking about is either a) a bit of a swiz – as just a lame mono functional device, or b) the actual correct and proper meaning of the words 'time machine' and thus making the use of those words to describe a device for enabling one to travel in time an absolute fraud!

Now I don't want to go off on a tangent (hate maths anyway – so I certainly wouldn't wanna journey anywhere on a sum) but surely that H G Wells bloke got it completely 'arse-about-face' when in 1895 he scribbled the ridiculously titled 'The Time Machine'. I mean ... I remember when reading this fucker's totally misleading novel for the very 1st time as a lad – I cried tears of complete emotional despair and despondency when I discovered that it actually wasn't an in-depth study of time pieces. Oh no, this pretty shitty and fraudulent book blooming ruined my day as well that first (and only) time I read it. I mean – there I was ... sat naked on the floor with my 'one-eyed-trouser-snake' grasped firmly in my hand and favourite 'wank-sock' by my side (for mopping up duties), ready for a thoroughly good read, followed by a timepiece fuelled orgasm. But oh no ... it was just some freaking far-fetched rubbish about this Edwardian twat in a posh chair stuck on a couple of planks of wood and with a few springs, coils and wires attached – that dreamt he'd travelled to the end of time and woke up to see the destruction of the world. And no doubt all cobbled together in his warped and child-like mind whilst clearly under the influence of Gin or a 19th century alcopop ... or something like that?

No wonder that blooming Wells bloke only used his initials and not his full name ... as clearly for fear of being exposed as a complete twit … err or charlatan who couldn't even title a book correctly. I'll bet his initials stood for Hapless Goon. I mean – what a complete knob-cheese … it should've been 'The Time Traveling Machine' … Mr Wells! Oh – and don't even mention freaking DeLoreans – or as my spell checker is telling me 'Delores' … as that's just plain stupid as cars can't travel through time either. Mine (a Ford I call Betty … hmmm?) struggles to get me the 4 miles to fucking work in the morning. Mind you – I work in the 'backwater' town of Ramsey – so maybe I am actually going back in time every day?

So quickly … back to the word 'frankly'. Why is it that this boy's name is used as a word meaning 'to be straightforwardly honest'? And anyhow – who was this Frank Ly – and what earth-shattering thing did he achieve to get a word named after his name? Now I'm actually gonna divert away from this as I'll have a rant dedicated to people's names at a later date … no really … I've already got some shit jotted down (like 'Carla' … grrr).

Oh and even quicker (honest) 'flying' (apt as you discover in a few secs) back to impossible and improbable … well okay – not really. But it did getting me thinking (which is a rare event … rarer than rocking horse shit) of that other imponderable … what's the difference between 'unlawful' and 'illegal'? Well (and I'm gonna hide behind the sofa whilst telling you the answer) … ones a sick bird!

Anyhow before I take a totally tedious detour into the whys, what's and whereabouts of imaginary rule books (or have I already just done that) I'd better crack (not literally) on with some subject matter that's actually worthy of a rant. And so, without further ado – what the friggin' hell's going on eh? I mean … what was up with the original method of 'closure'. Eh?

Why oh why is it that some clever boffins <<commonly used, but not really a word for white coat wearing scientists, word – Alert>> have to attempt to reinvent the wheel or worse still … fix something that ain't broken. Oh – and when I say reinvent the wheel – I don't actually mean to do it – as that's not possible … as wheels are just that … wheels … and they're not for turning – err which of course they are? Mind you – I suppose there are rollers and castors (not the oil variety) on the bottom of big wooden tables and chairs and TV cabinets … so maybe some boffins (yes them again) have already secretly reinvented the wheel and just stuck 'em on stuff … without telling us. Hmm?

So, anyhow going back to what I started to rant about … but actually didn't … 'closure'. And in particular … buttons. Well to be more precise … buttons on men's jeans. Who the heck came up with that gem of an idea? I mean what the duck (keeps on doing that 'Mr Goody-Two-Shoes' spellcheck … when I mean 'fuck') is wrong with the good old faithful zipper. Eh? I mean it's so easy and straight forward to use … down-swish and do what you wanna do and then when you've finished whatever it is you're doing … it's up-swish … and you're done. Modesty all protected and no 'crown jewels' or 'droopy danglers' … err dangling out of your pants in the wind.

Now to demonstrate the ridiculousness of buttons on men's jeans you have to look no further than a typical lad's night out. Imagine the scene … a bloke is out with his mates for a night out … and after quaffing <<excellent word for drinking quickly, word – Alert>> a good few scoops of the intoxicating brown stuff, that inevitable and fateful time comes when you have to go. And so you 'break the seal' – the first time you go for a pee on a night out … as once you go – you won't be able to stop! In fact, you'll be up and down like a 'whore's drawers' … pissing profusely all frigging night.

So back in the 'old days' you'd just go for a slash when the urge took ya – and when you were done – you'd simply stuff the old 'one eyed trouser snake' back into your undies and zip up and go. All done in the blink of an eye – well unless you'd catch the 'old man' in said zipper and then your eyes would water like a teething baby peeling onions (if they do … peel onions that is and not teeth – as even I know baby's do that … I was one once). Indeed – going for a pee used be so easy … a veritable 'slash in a flash'. It was a case of … stand, unzip, unfurl, point, pee, shake, shake again (as there's always that annoying little dribble), fold away, zip up, fart … and stroll off. That was sooo easy and even quicker if you didn't bother to wash your hands … I never do as they're always a bit splashed from the end of pee shaking action – and hey presto, I just have to rub my conveniently already wet hands together until dry. I mean water's water after all.

But oh no … all this simplicity has gone now and the common zipper – or in Latin, 'rapido-closicus-thy-gussetus' on men's jeans is alas – rarer than an Iguana in a leotard. And thus now days – going for a nice long slash on a busy weekend night out with the lads is so very difficult. I mean – now when the 'seal breaks' you've got to watch the door to the gents' toilets carefully like a friggin hawk and wait … and when you think that it's quiet in there – off you run – by now holding your crotch like it's about to explode and flood your pants. And why all the need to go to all this covert hassle?

Well it's simply this. Whilst these buttons are so very easy to undo when you arrive at the urinal to pee away … they're an absolute freaking ball ache to close! So when you've finished pointing 'Percy at the porcelain' or 'syphoning the python' … and you attempt to put your 'one eye trouser snake' back in your pants … you can't get the freaking things closed! Oh no! You start fumbling around like a blind man reading a book whilst wearing gloves and it's like your fingers are covered in grease and the stupid buttons are 3 times the size of the friggin button holes. And all this is intensified by the fact that you know that the other blokes in the bog are probably watching you thinking – 'What's that friggin weirdo doing? … He's either a) actually having a "five-knuckle-shuffle" and playing with himself, or b) he's hanging around in here trying to catch a "butchers" of my cock?' Not that I've done a) or b) mind … as I just go to the toilet to pee … well mostly. Hmm …!

Anyway – and it'll come as no surprise – I could rant on for ages and ages about 'over engineered' or new-fangled twists on perfectly working traditional devices … but hey … I'd end up boring the pants off you … and they'd be a bugger to put back on due to those stupid freaking buttons!

Oh … and if you're ever out in a bar and you meet me and I offer you a crisp – from a bag I'm already munching from … best not take me up on it and instead politely decline … well – that is unless you like salt 'n' my vinegar flavour!

Ostentatious Vulgarity Champions Arctic Hilarity!

I was listening to that 'Busted' (although it was actually in one piece?) song 'Year 3,000' the other night … oh yeah. You know the one … the one that bizarrely rambles on about how things are pretty much the same as they are now, in the 31st century … what with folk living under the sea, and which also (and oddly enough) makes reference to how healthy my great, great, great granddaughter is (I don't even have one … yet)?

Now before you switch off here and go and watch a tree grow … or something else more interesting … Busted were (as they've since split) truly great … and sorta world famous. I mean as well as this nonsense tune – Busted also penned the highly acclaimed (well by me at least) UK number 1 chart hit – 'What I go to school for'. Now this masterpiece, in case you didn't know (or care) … was all about a schoolboy's crush on his teacher – Miss Mackenzie, who in the pop-video was a) pretty hot, and b) showed her bra … which in my 'shallow-minded-typical-bloke' book – is all the ingredients required for a smash hit!

Oh – and before you read on – it's important to remember here that this ain't the Jonas Brothers (are they related or an 'order' of monks) 'cheap' and frankly pathetic copycat 'Year 3,000' cover-version (write your own songs you losers) … nope, this is the very crazy 'stiff upper lip' … well not really … British pop original. And therefore, you'd better take a quick 'butchers' at the following little link thingamajig to set the scene and get you really in the mood for the shite I'm shortly about to spout!

And so here it is … https://vimeo.com/108597642

Err … okay, so it was pretty catchy – but c'mon – it's totally and completely bananas … and if I'm brutally honest (which I am) a total pile of iguana poop! "So fair enough Quaggers … it is complete nonsense – but why does this randomness rile you so much," you'll no doubt be mumbling. "It's not like you could write any better – could you?" I hear you cry … (that's mumbling and crying now in quick succession – so get a grip gang). But oh yes … and to quote a famous Shakespeare rambling – 'definitely maybe!' Or was that that <<repeated words that are allowed to be right next to each other, words – Alert>> other Brit band, who were ridiculously named after a brother answering the question – 'what letter comes before B' – that his sister had just asked (think about it). Well, whatever – I'm actually gonna dedicate a whole rant to that bearded long dead playwright (Shakespeare and not a Gallagher brother), so it's straight back to Busted and those crazy lyrics and my apparent unqualified, or indeed qualified right to slate them.

So what's up with this and why does it trouble me? Well the simple problem, or rather problems with these lyrics are twofold. I mean, a) they're complete, unrealistic and improbable tosh, and b) yes I could do better and will prove so in a moment or two … or three. Now instead of just explaining what I'm on about by penning some random bullet points (why are they called that as they can't harm you can they, or fit in a gun … as they'd drip out of the barrel as they're made of ink), I'm actually gonna repeat the lyrics again – but substitute the bollox of Busted for my own words, which will be underpinned by realism … which if nothing else will fill a few lines of this rubbish. Oh … but hang about though – I think that before I attempt to rewrite this nonsense – I'd best first actually explain my complete bewilderment somewhat and then dive into my (possible) number one 'replacement' hit. So let's dissect a bit.

And so - that 1st line … well it's complete bollox really when you think about (and you don't even have to do so that hard) with its frankly ridiculous blasé reference to underwater living.

What the hell! Now if they'd said that they all minced <<a word describing a 'camp' walk in this context and not sliced and diced beef, word – Alert>> around in tin-foil kimonos, luminous sharkskin underwear and had shoes made of sautéed potatoes … then okay – that's plausible as being able to fall under the description of "not much has changed". But … "Living under water"! Now fuck me standing up and call me Mr Picky Pants – but surely the switch from living on land to total underwater habitation is a bloody fundamental and extremely significant change!

Then there's the ridiculously crazy, untrue and impossibly unrealistic (okay Quaggers … we get the drift) statement that refers to how healthy my child's, child's, child's, child's … daughter is. Do what? Now surely if it's actually 'your great, great, great granddaughter …' then she'd be 'brown bread' (dead). In fact, if it's the year 3,000, which it is as the song is entitled exactly that, then alas – the poor girl unfortunately died about 870 years ago. I mean, given

131

the normal life expectancy of a female … and even allowing for the adding of about 10 years' worth of longevity <<lovely longish word meaning – long-life, word – Alert>> for expected better health and medicines in the future … she'd still be long dead and 'curling up her toes' or 'pushing up the daisies' by the friggin year 3,000. So … and if you're talking reality here … then it should've been, 'And your great, great, great, great, great, great, great, great, great, great, great, great, great, great, great, great, great granddaughter is doing fine!' But hey, how ridiculous would that have sounded and anyhow it wouldn't have fitted into the song – as it's nearly one in its blooming self.

Nope … this is complete and utter bollox, as are most of the rest of the lyrics! And as such, this is how it should've been written … or how I'd have played it … err okay just written it – as I can't actually play a musical instrument. Well except the organ … mine!

And so …

"I've been to the 31st Century, and a significant amount of stuff has changed like people live under the sea, oh and the daughter of your great, great, grandson is alas - pretty dead!"

I'd of then somehow have fitted in an extra verse-chorus thingy – along the lines of … *'Now although that other long dead bint (aka your great, great, great granddaughter) is dust – I'm so very pleased to advise that your great, great, great, great, great, great, great, great, great, great, great, great, great, great, great, great, great granddaughter … is pretty fine (yeah pretty fine). In fact – she's doing really, really well and is a successful business person'* (gender-specifics are banned in the future as non PC) *'who owns and runs a*

132

very successful robotic-staffed mobile nail and hair salon and drives around in a 2 seater sports submarine-car with go faster fins, chauffeured by a seahorse named Colin'.

Nope ... I don't know what they were smoking when they penned these bonkers <<a word that in this context has nothing to do with sex, word – Alert>> lyrics, but hey ... it still reached number 2 in the UK pop charts so I suppose there must've been something of substance and appeal in it. Then again ... maybe, if they'd have asked me to write it, with my version of the lyrics – it would've reached No. 1 ... which is the only place to be (as to be No. 2 is to be the first of the losers). But alas it was what it was – and only God knows if it could've hit the top-spot with more sensible and realistic words?

Oh and talking of God ... have you ever been on a bus and found that God was sitting next to you, or a few rows in front ... or behind and dressed in a shabby sweat-stained white string vest, with his hairy pot belly resting awkwardly over his lap and his flabby ass hanging out of the top of a pair of ill-fitting tracksuit bottoms? No? I thought not ... and neither have I. So what's this gotta do with the price of bread? Well, although it's got absolutely nothing to do with how much a loaf costs ... I have to ask this seemingly odd question as I'm absolutely puzzled and perplexed (same thing – but another '2' to the word count) as to why that Canadian (think wannabe Americans) songstress Alanis Morissette had to warble about this nonsense in her hit pop tune 'One of Us'?

Well okay ... so actually she didn't ... and indeed never did ... as it's a very, very, very little known fact (or maybe it isn't – and I'm just living in a pop-fact-less bubble) that Ms. Morissette never actually released, or

133

even once sung the well-known song 'One of Us'. What … you say? Well – 'tis true! In fact, it was just bizarrely attributed to her by complete mistake. Now you might have to search a bit on Google (don't bother with Bing as he's just a long dead crooner) to discover that it was actually sung and released by a certain Ms. Joan Osbourne. Who? Indeed – but you know what … I don't care, as it's the crackers lyrics that I'm moving on to … right now!

So – 'One of us'. Now I'm a massive fan of the big Guy/Gal with the long grey hair – and have got all his/her … err book, but I have to wonder what it would be like if he/she was actually just one of us? Now you might think that's ridiculous as he's/she's God and we're us. So how could he/she be one of us unless we were one of him/her and he's/she's not and we're not? Eh? But if that's the case (and it is – as I'm not God and he/she's not me … as if I was then how come I ain't yet won the lottery yet) then why did that looney Alanis Morissette write and sing that whacko song about it with those ridiculous lyrics. I mean – did she know the Busted guys? Oops … now I know it actually wasn't her that wrote or sung the song – but alas I've already forgotten what the other real-singer lady was called … so, err – lets quickly look at the words!

Well okay, so I actually can't remember precisely how the lyrics go as I've got a head like an old sieve … but it was something along the lines of … 'imagine if the big all-seeing white haired geezer up in heaven actually was just some fat, untidy, lost looking bloke on a bus?' Now what the fuck … how (and for the 2nd time in one rant) bonkers is that?

Now before I move into this final phase of this lyrically challenged rant I'm gonna end this PC shite about God's gender right here. Now God is a bloke, a man … a guy. Fact! I mean if God was a girl then they'd be called Godette … and they ain't! So there!

And so God. I mean – firstly … what the fuck was he doing on a bus? Isn't he supposed to be able to fly … or was that Superman or another superhero? I know it wasn't Batman, as crazily enough he (and unlike the name incorrectly suggests) couldn't actually fly … unlike a bat which can … well unless it's the cricket or baseball variety – which then of course … can't.

And how come he was a slob … is that 'cos he took the bus everywhere – when he could've flown and actually exercised … well his arms at least? And why did she compare him to 'a slob like one of us'? I'm not a slob! Okay … so I like slouching around on the sofa eating slices of pizza wearing just my underpants … and a bib (me wearing the pants by the way and not the pizza of course as that would be crazy) … but I also like to work-out … and no I don't mean work out how many pizzas I can eat in an hour. And anyhow even if I was a slob … how does bleeding Morissette (err I mean Osbourne) know? I mean she's never even met me … well not so I remember! It's a blooming cheek – that's what it is I tell you … to falsely assume and label 'us' as slobs. And is she insinuating that all people who ride on buses are lazy and fat! That's complete bollox isn't it – well except for the bus drivers – as they're all complete lard-asses! Believe me … you'll never see a thin one. Fact!

Oh and what about the lyrics 'trying to find his way home' … Eh? How come? Now I'm not the biggest religious person in the world (as in only 5'10" and 12 stones) but even I know they he lives in heaven … and where that is. I mean you don't need bloody GPS (don't know what that means – but I guess it's not a group of doctors) or 'Satnav' (meaning to locate places whilst sitting down?) to find your way to heaven. Oh no … you either just have to die and you're there instantaneously, or if your still in the land of the living, then you just look up in the sky on a clear day and hey presto – there it is! You know … just left of the far side of the moon. Isn't it? Or is that the international space station? Whatever – God must blooming well know, as it's his home and he's God. I mean – if God knows everything about everything – which he does (well except the winning lottery numbers obviously), then surely he must know where he flipping lives … and not have to rely on some lardy-assed bus driver dropping him off at his doorstep!

Nope – I'm afraid this is just another blooming cars (typed 'case' there … my right finger's getting tired now) of these so-called pop stars taking flipping liberties and producing piles of meaningless literary poop. I mean what gives some people the right to believe that they can get away with just churning out complete utter bollox and think that others would be interested in it. Eh?

Oh and very finally (honest) – and going back to the gender thing I 'skirted' (apt) around back there a bit with that God bloke … what the fuck's going on with Alanis Morissette anyway? Is she a really lady or a bloke pretending to be a lady? I ask as it's a bit of a strange first name isn't it? I mean was she born a boy and always wanted to be a girl and so changed her boy's name to a girl's one … but wasn't very imaginative? Or was she actually born a girl but her parents wanted a boy and in refusing to accept it cryptically hid their frustrations in naming her? I mean … Alan is Morissette … or is she/he?

Mr Ichthyosaurus and the Potato Fence Poseidon Gang!

Oh no I hear you say … and actually, I can 'hear you say' – as I've got bionic fucking ears!

Now apologies for the swear word there which a) is totally unlike me and b) absolute bullshit as my lugholes are neither bionic or possess the ability to fornicate! Ooh – 'fornicate' I hear you purr inquisitively … well I love this word but rarely 'do' it – err I mean 'use' it! Even better than the word though (go on whisper it to yourself 10 times without smiling like an over happy hyena having its feet tickled) … is its actual official meaning.

'Fornicate'. Verb. Meaning … 'Upper class fuckery, or more especially, a word designed to roll off the tongues of royalty' … e.g.

King: "My dear Queen, whist the footman fucks the maid, shall we retire to the royal fornication chamber?"

Now, I bet you never knew the real meaning before did you – and will no doubt try to bring 'fornicate' into your everyday conversations from now on. I know I will!

Hey – and whilst on the subject of the word fornicate (told you I'd use it) … and 'fucking' ears – imagine two things here.

137

1. How desperately unfortunate would it be if you were a female royal nymphomaniac and your name was Kate. You'd be asked by the king, or prince or … err … milkman – "Excuse me, m'lady – but would you like to fornicate, Kate?" You'd think that every blinking sexual suitor had a frigging stutter … although I suppose on the the (see it's spreading) plus side … you'd get plenty of action!

And (and you're gonna have to totally regress into Quaggers' crazy world here) …

2. Imagine if your ears really could fornicate. Wow! I mean you'd possess more sexual organs than you'd know what to do with … and you'd be capable of having 'ear-sex'! How wacky and delightful would that be … eh? Maybe … although not to be confused with the similarly sounding 'Essex' … which as we all know is a part of England where everyone where's sunglasses in winter, drives a purple Golf GTI with tinted windows and talks like they've … err … just had ear-sex! I mean, you could rub and caress each other's ears using your hands, or ears … for ear to ear sex. You could even use your 'one-eyed trouser snake' – but hey – only if you're a bloke … oh, and used some form of 'lube' – like 'Swarfega' (you might wanna Google it … or maybe not) – as ear holes are pretty tiny … even for the most 'challenged' of gentlemen.

You could even use your feet for toe to ear foreplay and erotic merriment.

Or of course you could just play with your own … and partake in the practice of <<New Word Alert>> 'mast-ear-bating'. Hmm!

And hey, a whole new industry could be created employing thousands – making 'safe ear-sex protection' in the form of ear condoms ... or even an ear pill ... to pop in your ear just to make doubly sure in case the ear-rubber slipped off or split ... and the ear wax – went where it wasn't wanted!

A further industry could also be created making ear-underwear because as fornication objects, they'd be sexually explicit and as such be desired and erotic parts of the body that would have to be kept in private in case you got arrested for (and you're gonna groan) ... 'Ind-ear-cent' exposure! Another <<New Word Alert>> ... fuck me you're getting your money's worth here. In fact, the only place you could expose them in public would be on nudist ear beaches ... or 'nudist b-ear-ches!' Now I won't mention another New Word Alert there as you'll be getting bored of that by now ... oh dang.

Hmm – perhaps I need some more of my 'med-ear-cation' ... you've gotta love it. Hey maybe I should submit these new words to the Oxford English Dictionary ... or wait for it ... to 'Wikip-ear-dia'! I'll think I should stop this now ... right now.

Anyhow ... "It's that fuckwad Garfield Quaglioni again," I hear you say (again) ... "When the freaking heck in God's name will this complete Viking twonk stop spouting utter iguana shite?" Now actually (and I shit you not ... but to divert you from the fact that it is indeed me again spouting bollox) ... my real 1st name is Garfield and my real surname is Quaglioni. Now as for 'Garfield' ... I know what you're thinking ... but I wasn't in fact named after a chunky furry ginger pussy. Not that there's anything wrong with them like, as I for one are quite partial to a bit of chunky furry ginger pussy ... err ... forget I said that and please – don't tell the 'tripubkljsi sdd stftrethat'! I actually typed 'trouble and strife' (wife) there, but I my fat-rudderless fingers inexplicably switched into Serbian type-font there.

So, where was I – oh yeah, Garfield. Well I'm called this simply as I was conceived in a car, parked in a field. Yup! Mum chose the 'field' part and Dad, who was a big car fanatic chose the 'Gar' part … alas he was a shit speller!

Oh … and whilst on the subject of big pussys (we are honest) – I was at the airport last week returning home from vacation and I was going through security when this really, really large lady in the queue in front of me got stopped and whisked away by the police. I later found out that she'd been arrested for drug smuggling! Apparently they found 60lb of crack in her knickers!

Soo … and quickly back to the paragraph or two before. And as for the Quaglioni part of my name well that's simple as the car I was conceived in was Italian – a Fiat … oh, and just like the lovable big cat who I wasn't name after … they loved lasagne. No imagination my parents! Mind you, I say that … but maybe whilst their scope of imagination might've been somewhat limited (my brothers called 'Neil' … no not 'Kneel' or something creative like that … just plain old 'Neil'), their sense of humour was not! Oh no, I've had to live with my middle name 'Willy' all my life – although it's a lot easier now that I'm grown up and the references to being called 'little Willy' have ceased. No really.

But hang on though, is my name not really just 'Gary Quaggan' and I've simply wasted half a digit full of finger ink typing this total pap … … ermm, actually yes!

Anyway, and after a good few paragraphs of total trampoline tosh … it's me again and I'm fully 'back in the room'. As such, and just like my hero – the legend

140

that is Miley Cyrus -recently warbled on her hot record – oops I meant to type 'hit' there … 'We can't stop … and we won't stop!' So I won't … err … stop.

She is hot mind … not like the sun though or a really hot curry or like when you burn your ear on the iron whilst ironing and the phone rings … and then when you burn your other ear when 5 minutes later it rings again! But she is a hottie though. Oh and whilst we're talking about ironing – I wonder if posh British actor Jeremy Irons actually does … or does Irons not iron? So quickly back to the queen of music. Now I really do love Miley Cyrus, but what a really silly first name. I mean – what were her parents smoking when they came up with that corker! Why name their daughter after a unit of distance measurement? All I can say is … it's a freaking good job she was born in the US under the imperial measurement system as opposed to in Europe and under the nonsense metric one. I mean how incredibly ridiculous would it have been and how famous would she ever have become named 'Kilometery'!

Oh and as for her surname – well that's just freaking pretentious. I mean why take the name of an odd-shaped Mediterranean island – and then just arrogantly drop the 'P'? Fuckers they are!

Now you might be scoffing and dismissing my claim that Miley's a legend. Well in my mind (accepted it's tinier that the left testicle of a juvenile ant suffering from dwarfism) she is probably the greatest musician ever. I mean she's right up there (or even better) with the other legends of rock and pop like:

The Beatles (they were men),

The Rolling Stones (just men too),

Abba – or abbA backwards – which actually translates to 'a public bar' in Swedish (honest). And … of course,

The Pet Shop Boys. Who I hear you ask … who? Google 'em – they're awesome … err … well … 'ish'!

Oh – and on this theme – well okay I'm lying as it's a totally different theme … A female legendary popstar bought a pair of really old and tatty second-hand binoculars for $5000 earlier this week … I think the bloke in the shop must've seen her coming a Miley away!

So finally (really), and this will come as no surprise as you've by now no doubt realized that I'm a total 'loon' and so thick that I make pig shit look like a professor of quantum physics with a further degree in economics, but … I've decided to change my name to a more suitable one – as you'll probably agree.

And therefore from now on I'll be using the surname 'Kerr' and the 1st name of 'Wayne'!

Hey it could've been worse though as I could've decided on other new names like … 'Betty Swollocks', 'Mike Hunt', 'Willy Sanker', 'Billy Sastard' or 'Hugh Janus'!

And so very finally (I lied before) … you probably didn't know this personal fact about me – but as we're now really good friends I'll spill the beans – I actually suffer from Insomnia. But hey – I look on the bright side … I've only got 3 sleeps till Christmas!

Preponderance Spanners of Dalliance Melts Banners?

Horsey, horsey don't you stop,

    Just let your feet go clippity-clop,

    Your tail goes Swish,

    And the wheels go round,

    Giddy up we're homeward bound!

Yup – this week I've got the trots.

Now when I say 'trots' I don't of course mean – the 'Trotsky's' – aka 'jelly-botty' or 'loose-ass' syndrome. Oh no. In fact … I actually mean that I've got the trots … the ones that horses have. You know, as they 'trot' about when they can't be arsed running … and not of course when they've got dodgy bum flaps and have to trot off on a regular basis to the lavatory (if they're house-trained … and if not … the corner of a field – just over the 'blind-side' of the hedge where they can easily be stood in). And anyhow that would be the trots-trots … and this week I'm only talking about a singular 'trots' … or to cut a very (and it is) long story a tad shorter … 'horses'.

Oh – and before I fence (I typed 'delve' there and aren't about to challenge you to a sword fight) into horses … I'd better just quickly flick back to that (on the face of it) bizarre opening paragraph … which quaintly <<old fashioned and ambient, word – Alert>> and as you might've spotted … rhymed. Well … that's an old Manx (natives of the Isle of Man) folk song sung for about 120 years now … although not continually as a) that would be impossible – unless there was at least 50 or more of you as you'd need to take regular breaks to eat, drink, sleep, shower (or bath if you prefer) and wee and poop and b) you'd have to be very, very young (like minus 40yrs) when you started singing and strictly adhered to a very healthy diet of total bad-stuff abstinence … to live for 100+ years! Now you might be thinking that it's not possible to be a minus age like -40? Well, it is. I mean we're all already 9 months old when we pop our heads out and say hello to the world for the 1st time aren't we. And as we don't start the 'age clock' ticking from 0 until we're out and about and wriggling around and crying and peeing and pooing and gurgling and farting … then the fact is … that at birth you're already ¾ of a year old … or minus 9 months! Now how you could stretch that to minus 40yrs to be able to sing for 120 years … is beyond my pea-like brain and maybe pushing it a bit … as I don't think a pregnancy has ever lasted that long? Not even for a tortoise … and they're as slow as fuck at everything they do … takes them wrinkly necked fuckers a day to have a shit … Err, I'll bet … although I can't claim to actually have observed.

Anyhow – and quickly 'back in the room' please Quaggers – this folk song was penned (or quilled if pens weren't invented back then) and sung in dedication to the Isle of Man's world famous (Err maybe) 'Douglas Promenade Horse Trams' which have been running since

1st May 1876 (this is BTW the only useful fact you're going to get in this rant – and even then I'm not sure if it's actually that useful).

Now – these ridiculously named 'horse trams' still run today in the summer months and don't, as their name clearly and indisputably suggests, carry horses. And therein lies possibly one of history's biggest miscarriages of incorrect-naming-justice (Err … maybe). Now you might be thinking – WTF here – but hey, let's just look at this in comparison with other similar named modes of transport. I mean (I say these two words a lot at the beginning of a sentence) … look at 'people carriers' … what do they carry Eh? Well it ain't friggin' (or even not sexually aroused) horses or giraffes wearing flip-flops or even genetically modified post boxes with hallucinogenic legs. Nope … it's friggin' people (again not sexually aroused). Then there's 'police cars' – they carry, as the mane (meant to type 'name' there – but hey relevant with current topic) police officers – nothing else.

Oh – and what about 'car transporters' … yup they carry cars and not Tiffany lampshades or lime green asparagus cuckoo clocks.

And hey … even 'fish tanks' – and although not a mode of piscine (Google it … I had to) armoured transport, actually contain – yes you've guessed it … fish.

Ooh – and what about an 'oil tanker', yup it carries oil and not reinforced concrete teapots; and a 'milk lorry' … yes – it's milk and not horses or fire-resistant pillows for caterpillars (if there are such things)?

So why does a 'horse tram' carry people and not freaking horses. Eh? Why isn't it called a 'people tram'?

Eh? Oh no that would be too freaking sensible! Mind you there is of course a 'school bus' which, okay doesn't actually carry 'schools' as that would be ridiculous and hey … they tend to stay put where they were built!

And finally (honest – for this bit anyhow) there is of course – 'taxi cabs' – which don't carry around other fee charging cars!

So anyway – and back to these so called 'horse trams' … they actually carry lazy people – posing as 'old-fashioned-transport-enthusiast-tourists' from one end of Douglas promenade to the other – which is the impossibly unimaginable walking distance of 1.5 miles. Now this might sound like a long way to walk to you – but it ain't … it's merely a stroll … and surely could be accomplished without having to coerce the services of a tram pulled by a horse. I mean let's not forget that everywhere is within walking distance – if you got the time!

So horses. Now don't get me wiring ('wrong' I typed there), I'm not 'horsist' or 'horsophobic' <<double made up words – Alert>> but what the fuck's the point of horses. Eh?

I mean – okay, say 100 years ago – and for a few odd thousand years before that … they served a purpose as a necessary but impractical and uncomfortable means of getting from A to B. That said although no one ever mentions and history has even forgotten those poor fuckers who in ancient times tried to get from C to D … or E to F. And as for those poor unheardofs <<new and made up, but should be a word, word – Alert>> folks who were trying to get from Y to Z … well, I don't know whatever happened to those poor fools? I mean what did they use for transport … no horses for them –

as that was only for those A to Bs … and maybe B to Cs. So did they just walk (or 'Shanks's Pony' as the Irish would say) … mind you – that's a kind of horse – so maybe they didn't use their own feet at all … and in fact all rode small horses purchased from some bloke called 'Shanks'! Who knows … who cares … well I do, but I'd better press on.

Oh – and when I said impractical – and uncomfortable – well you can only begin to try and imagine which unbelievably demented and misguided crazy fool thought that the best and most effective way for man to get around was to be sat astride a blooming horse. I mean look at the blinking 'in your face' evidence. Horses are like 5ft wide and our leg span is … well about 2ft. Okay more if you do the splits – but how many gymnasts or yoga enthusiasts did you ever see riding horses. Eh? None that's how many. And they're like 6ft off the freaking ground … if you had vertigo then you'd be well fucked! Now surely biggish dogs like a St. Bernard or even a small bear – like a panda would've be more practical. Mind you it's probably a good job that pandas weren't used as imagine how daft the WWF logo would look if it was one with someone sitting on its back … all credibility lost!

But hey – none of those options had seats, headrests or places to put your feet anyhow – so why didn't those clueless ancients just invent the car … or motorcycle? No wonder they were so behind the times … I mean you show me someone who can't invent a simple petrol engine and I'll show you a caveman!

But hey, that was then – and this is now. I mean 'old man' Shanks is probably long dead and we've had cars like forever now. Well ever since the automobile (to give its proper title) was invented by the famous but secretive

Welshman 'Ivor Car' ... I kinda might've made that last bit up. Now I might have to rant about cars in a later ... err rant ... as they're a worthy of at least 3 pages of bollox.

And so horses have really – if I'm brutally honest – have just become so surplus to requirements – and in reality ... nothing but a blinking nuisance. I mean nobody even rides horses these days – well except for a few posh people who in all honesty really only use this as an 'outlet' excuse for their domination fetishes! I mean look at the clues ... shiny knee high leather boots, leather (again) whips and excruciatingly tight elasticated beige trousers called 'jodhpurs' ... named after the Eskimo lady who 1st invented them as a means of keeping penguin meat fresh ... 'Jo Dhpurs' (really).

And of course the only other people that have any use for horses these days are those testosterone fuelled fools who live in Texas and who wear silly hats ... to go with their once again ... kinky leather boots!

Oh – and sorta finally – how really weird or stupid (or both) are horses anyhow – that they don't apparently feel pain in their toe nails. Now I mean surely their hoofs <<love that word – but don't know why, word – Alert>> are just really big ugly thick toenails – that – you'd think would have at least a modicum <<crazy Latin word that means little, word – Alert>> of sensitivity to pain. But oh no. I mean when these 'equine' (Latin again) sorts get a new pair of shoes they go through a ridiculous rigmarole whereby they don't just choose a nice shiny pair and slip them on ... they frigging have metal ones nailed onto their frigging feet! Now I'm no horse expert (or an expert in anything come to think of it) but even I know that I'd flipping well feel it if someone hammered nails into my plates (of meat).

Nope – these silly horses are totally a waste of time and these days should be consigned to just moping around in fields, eating straw and mints whilst wearing a floppy hat with holes for their ears … or is that donkeys – which of course are just dwarf horses. A bit harsh you might think – well in my opinion no. In fact, I think they should simply be outlawed – or at the least made to work for a living … like, err … pulling trams full of people.

Well that's about my spleen vented for another week or two and I'd better sign off for now and go and feed 'Flossie' … my beautiful old Shire horse. Eh?

Recalcitrant Ants Swap Horse-Shoes for Pants!

So … I was going to talk to you today about one of my two favourite subjects. Now my 1st favourite topic of conversation is 'Me' and the 2nd one is … err – well that's me as well! Now that's not because I'm vain – oh no, it's simply because I'm quite frankly a simpleton and it's the only subject that I really know anything about … I've been studying it all my life.

Anyhow – I decided against that and so it's swiftly on to my 5th favourite subject … (I'll cover 3rd and 4th another time in another rant) … and that's not a promise, it's a threat.

And so do you know what … I really do feel so sorry for dogs and cats. I mean it must be so truly awful for them not being able to choose their own name or names (if they've got a middle one). How bad must that be eh? And frustrating as well … particularly if they don't actually like the name that's been allocated to them by 'You' – or the person that you got them off. Or the person that you got them off, got them off! I mean, imagine if you've got a dog called 'Rex' (male dog or 'dog' – dog … unless of course you're a pet naming weirdo) and all along he'd rather be a 'Rover'. Now you might think he's all fine and dandy with his lot … but secretly he could actually be really pissed at you for giving him his 'non-name of choice'. Oh yeah … you might think he's side-smiling at you (like they do) but in reality it's an inverted growl – as it really gets right on his tits (well if he had any of course – which he wouldn't as he's a 'dog-dog') every time you call him it. Unbeknown to you – he might actually disappear off shortly after every time you call him 'that' name and go and punch a wall or even worse – kick or knee the cat … have dogs got knees? I mean – have you ever seen a dog punch a wall or kick a door … or knee a cat in the groin (cats do have groins BTW – but only if they're male and haven't had the 'snip') … well have you? Well okay … neither have I … but I'll bet my bottom dollar (if I had one – which I don't as we use £'s here) that they do this out of sight of you every single time you call them their name. Hey, I'll bet that they even swear as well whilst taking their frustration out on said wall, door … cat, and quietly bark under their doggy breath – doggy profanities directed at you – like 'Boner Head' or 'Two-Legged-Twat' or 'Cat Loving Wanker' or even 'Poodle Botherer'. I'll bet this shit really happens … as there's no scientific proof that it doesn't is there … eh!

And be sooo very, very careful to give them a clear and correct 'gender name' … unless of course you're sharing your life and home with one of those naturally 'gay' breeds of dog – like a Poodle or a Chihuahua. Oh yes, it's scientifically proven (well it might be) that these breeds of dog are actually quite gay … in fact – as 'gay as a maypole' wearing a pink dress on a marshmallow futon. Anyway … if you've got a 'dog' poodle or 'dog' Chihuahua then you've actually got a 'bitch' – and vice versa! No, really!

Now you might not have ever been aware of a particular and really strange phenomenon <<great word,

151

but not entirely sure what it means, word – Alert>> before (you will from now on) but 'dog' Poodles and 'dog' Chihuahuas are always hanging around outside beauty salons grooming themselves and looking at their nails. You'll also notice that they're constantly admiring themselves and looking at their reflections in ponds or really shiny car doors … or even standing on their hind legs balancing in front of (or against if they're tired against) wall mounted mirrors. As for 'bitches' of these breeds – well you'll (from now on) notice them hanging around garages and paying close attention and sniffing motorcycles parked on the road. You'll also be shocked, neigh stunned … when the realization smacks you right in the face that supposed 'bitches' these doggy breeds actually have a lot of facial hair and even beards – proof beyond doubt that they're more 'butch' than bitch! It'll also now become abundantly clear to you that these breeds actually walk in a girly (if a dog) or butch (if a bitch) manner … 'mincing' or 'stomping'! So next time you see Poodle or Chihuahua walking down the street … you won't need to slide underneath it to tell its gender … (best not anyway) … just observe its gait.

<<*A Rare 'Quaggers' Educational Alert*>>

'Gait' is the pattern of movement of the limbs of animals, including humans, during locomotion over a solid substrate (a surface or layer).

Oh and don't even talk about King Charles Spaniels – they're not they're queens!

Anyway – it's best therefore to stick with clear gender names that can't be mistaken – you know … like 'Clive' for a boy dog or 'Susan' for a girl dog or bitch. Best to avoid ambiguous <<clever word for I'm not actually clear, word – Alert>> names like Charlie or

Sam ... as these can cause confusion and perhaps a degree of sexual anguish to your furry friends. Oh – quick rewind back to the word 'ambiguous' ... I really like this word but it just doesn't do what it 'says on the tin' ... does it? I mean its sounds like it's the word for describing a large piece of meat that comes from a pig that is suitable for just one person or a few people! It's not. It's just so confusing ... which of course its meaning is.

We just don't really know what goes on in a doggy's head do we ... so always give more than just a thought when naming them, and call them it a few times and see what facial reaction you get. If they smile and wag their tails – you've got a doggy thumbs up – you're 'cooking on gas'. However, if they walk off around the corner growling – then they're no doubt kicking or punching something – so you'd best think again. Of course, if they just stand there looking stupid – then they're deaf. Mind you, we named one of our doggies Smudge ... which can be a dog or a bitch name. Luckily for us ... Smudge is a hermaphrodite ... so she's/he's not actually that bothered ... well not that we're aware of ... although there are a few low-down dents in some of the walls in our house – just above skirting board level. Oh and if you're not sure what a hermaphrodite is then just check (discretely) your lower regions ... and f you've got both sets of 'bits' ... then you're one!

Hey, and I nearly forgot about cats – as I did say that I felt sorry for both dogs and cats. Well the truth is that you actually don't need to worry too much about your feline friends, as they'll be far too busy – being 'kneed' in the groin or kicked by their 'pissed off' doggy brother or sister – to be bothered what the hell you call them. And anyhow ... all cats really care about is sitting on your lap licking themselves and purring and coughing up balls of fur. That and scratching holes in your carpets, furniture and curtains

And nearly-finally, as my right index finger is now quite literally about to run out of bullshit ink, I must mention a really weird thing that got me a pondering and a bit paranoid even – if I'm truthful. I heard an advert on the radio the other day that was 'carping' (although nothing to do with trout) on about a 'Great New Meal Deal' available at a 'McDonalds near you'! What the fuck? I mean how the friggin hell do they know where I live ... eh?

Oh, and really-finally, fear thee not as, as promised in a previous (or future rant), I still plan to talk about 'Jabba The Hut', the French, legendary Brit boy-band 'The Wanted', Shakespeare and other random stuff that although sit outside of my top 5 favourite things ... still matter to me. I'll cover these off in other instalments of my nonsense (no really), so be prepared for those little gems – whenever they pop up and bite you on the literary ass!

Stratospheric Demands Slope Forsaken Left Hands?

I had to cook my own dinner last night!

Oh yeah …

Now in order that you fully appreciate the gravity of this particularly traumatic (no really) and thoroughly unpleasant situation – I thought about offering you a more explanatory explanation (what?) and as such rephrase it and add a bit more detail in. But do you know what (and call me 'bone idle') … I've decided instead just to repeat it.

And so …

I had to cook my own dinner last night.

Oh bollox … I've just realized that I didn't actually' repeat' that last bit as the 1st one had an exclamation mark at the end and this latest one's only gotta a full stop – which as well as being a different symbol thingy – is only about a third as meaningful. Oh yeah. I mean the common-a-garden (what?) sentence-ending or acronym separating 'full' stop is actually worth only 33.333333% of the point's value of an exclamation mark … which is way more expressive and important! But anyway – enough of this English grammatical point's value nonsense … as do these symbols even have scores? I think not.

Now bizarrely enough (and so totally random even for me) I've just had that movie 'The Maze Runner' creep into my cavernous but empty mind … but akygiyhj (I actually typed 'although' there) it's a great film … it's not actually worthy of a rant … so thankfully for you … I'll park it and move on. But of course I may one day eventually come back to the subject of 'movies' in a future rant (or a previous one – depending on in which order you're reading this series of shite) and then you'll be able to read all about actors/actresses (why aren't they called 'actoresses'?), gaffers, credits, stuntmen and 'best-boys'. Or of course maybe you've already read it … that is of course if I've actually penned it – which only you (yes you … oh and maybe God) will know if you read it previously. Now if you haven't read a Movie focused Quaggers pants-rant, then you've got 3 possible scenarios facing you. Either:

1. I did write it and your order of Pantsrantians reading has yet to let you stumble upon it.

2. I didn't write it and as such you're never gonna have to suffer the misfortune of stumbling across it.

Or,

3. I did write it and it was so soporific (google it – but it's just a biggish clever word that's bollox really) that when you awoke you simply forgotten you'd read it!

Oh – now although I might've given the firm impression back there a bit that I wouldn't be revisiting the aforementioned English grammatical stuff, (as that's a totally different 'kettle of fish' than the main topic which I really want to ramble on about this time), I've just gotta conduct a very brief (it won't be) archaeological dig (it isn't) into this correct punctuational nonsense.

And so … here we go … I'll start digging (not really)! Now where the friggin fuck do these ridiculously entitled 'Proper English' words/symbols actually get their names from? I mean was the bespectacled (gotta be … they all are … I know I am) clever dick who named English grimmer (Freudian slip as meant 'grammar') symbols actually an Alien from the planet 'Booblebottiliterix-Fleurp'? And why did he, or she … or it, have to invent them. What's up with unpunctuated or less formal grammar … eh? Surely if our ancient caveman relatives only needed to grunt to communicate effectively and achieve stuff like getting their friggin dinner made for them … (grrr), or ironing done for them – then why the need to over bloody complicate matters nowadays? I mean if we quickly look at some examples – you'll soon be raising a Quagger's 'point well-made appreciation' flag up the flagpole and saluting it! Maybe even whilst naked in further and absolute appreciation … err … or maybe not!

So here's a few English Grammatical words that really sound like (and actually are) complete nonsense and that in all honesty aren't even worth a wank in a sports shop:

Commas … a word to describe long deep sleeps?

Apostrophes – a word for some ancient Greek Mathematical God (boy could they do with him now)?

Colon – a body part?

Semi Colon – half a body part?

Question Mark – an inquisitive bloke?

Inverted Comma – a shy person in a deep sleep?

Now if there's an inverted one – why is there's an extroverted comma … eh? You know – a comma that's likes to dress in designer clothes and wear loads of bling and drive around in flash cars ... err ... whist in a deep sleep? Nowhere ... that's where! In fact, I'm beginning to wonder if English isn't as much a complete waste of freaking time as that Latin bollox ... which as you know ... really grips my shit!

And so back to my cooking my dinner ... well actually not just yet ... as hang in there for one additional dang minute. I must just flash (not literally as my knob and baubles get cold and shrink up when I do that) back to the previous mention of a 'kettle of fish'. Well a kettle anyhow ... as fish are for a future or indeed a previous rant as well. So ... how come is it that when you boil a kettle and make a nice hot cup of tea – you fill a cup 5 6ths full of boiling water and add only 1 6th of cold milk ... you're then immediately able to take a refreshing sip or two? I mean how come it doesn't burn you're friggin lips off you're friggin face and heat shrink your blooming tongue ... eh? I mean the water's so piping hot when it comes out of the kettle – it makes the centre of the Sun seem like the inside of a fridge ... well except for the in (and out of) date food-stuff that's lurking in there? Nope, to me it's a complete freaking conundrum <<not a word for a convict that's just removed a percussion instrument from a band, word – Alert>> that's basically unfathomable ... but perhaps arguable as to whether it actually deserved a mention in this rant.

And talking about the Sun (we just did ... honest), that reminds me that the Irish Space Agency, 'P. I. S. S' (Paddy's in Spacecraft Situations) have just announced that they're sending an exploratory mission to the sun. Irish astronauts Patrick Fitzwilliam and William

Fitzpatrick (they're in a civil partnership) plan to set off at night – so they won't get burned!

Oh and please just this one final, final, final (3 x finals = definitely) time forgive me for yet another brief digression (and I promise tis the last one ever … well in this rant) as I wanna go – and very rapidly pinch the backside of the phrase – 'bone idle' which I mentioned lightyears ago in paragraph one. Now what a ridiculously silly saying that is, as bones simply aren't. I mean they're anything but as they're always bloody moving about – you know, like your arms and your legs … okay and accepted with the aid of skin, flesh, muscles and blood … and stuff. Unless of course you're brown-bread! Mind you – of course an actual 'boner' is totally different as although it's not a real bone – I suppose for some unfortunates it can be completely idle … and therefore the name is apt! Of course the phrase might have just become misspelt over time and was originally 'bone idol' and meant to describe some ancient talent competition for skinless limbs who could sing a bit … you know like that Pop Idol nonsense? Maybe …

And so finally (and eventually) it's back to my dinner and my unbelievable and totally unfair need to cook it! So what's the problem with you cooking your own dinner I hear you mumble? Well it's just not right is it? I'd even go as far to say that it was so fundamentally wrong, inappropriate and in all honesty a crime against 'mankind'. I'm actually surprised I wasn't stuck down right where I stood (in the kitchen with a little apron on – with 'Bake My Day' adorned across the front) by some testosterone fuelled Man-God, like err that Thor bloke with the big hammer … for being such a girlie!

I mean cooking … well it's women's work isn't it! Note an exclamation mark and not a question mark. It's just like that ironing and cleaning and washing-up and doing the laundry … you know, tasks that are meant for women to do. I mean the evidence is clearly there for all to see as:

1. Women's hands are purposefully shaped to precisely hold domestic utensils and appliances – like ladles, pots and pans, whisks, irons, kettles, dusters, mops and brooms and so on …

And,

2. It categorically (maybe) states in the Bible that (and I quote) 'God created woman in the image of his old mom (whose steak and potato pies – BTW – were legendary) and that she shalt thou cook and clean and wash for him as he was … a-men (groan)!'

Now okay – I'll come clean with you and admit that I've not actually read the Bible in its entirety … although I have studied the index once or twice and know who the main 'characters and players' are! But I'll bet you 50 pence … or maybe a pound that it says something like that in there as surely God wouldn't have had to rustle up his own spaghetti Bolognese for dinner after a busy day of parting oceans and teaching his son how to make cheap wine out of sea water and other equally impressive stuff involving fish and bread, immortality and waking up perfectly fine after having gotten absolutely hammered the previous day. Erm – I'll move on …

Oh – and could you ever imagine him dancing around heaven cleaning the clouds with a Hoover … whilst donning a flower emblazoned piny and listening to Bohemian Rhapsody through ridiculously oversized headphones? No of course you can't … as either him old mom or Mrs God (if he was married) would've done all that domestic stuff for him ... whilst he busied himself with imaginative and important stuff like creating gardens full of nude people, talking persuasive snakes and fruit that was seriously bad for your health!

Now before you go and grab a big stick and a flaming torch (AA battery one's don't have the same impact) to come and get and punish me (like those mobs in them old movies) for being a raging sexist – I'm actually not. Nope – I'm certainly not a male chauvinist and in fact I don't have a sexist bone in my body ... although I'm quite hot ... and do have a, err ... sexy bone? But, I am married and as such I've always been an advocate of the saying – 'if you've got a dog, don't bark yourself'! Ouch! ... and fuck me backwards ... arghh ... my wife has just read that last bit and my nuts are now throbbing uncontrollably in immense and excruciating pain!

She's left the room now so I shall continue – albeit with an ice pack on my 'crown-jewels'.

And so – let's face it, cooking in particular is really women's work and men should only ever have to cook on two special occasions – at barbecues and at Christmas. It's a well-known fact that women can't cook barbecues as they can't light the blooming things! Sure women can switch on a hob, cooker or even a microwave oven. But give them anything more challenging, like getting friggin charcoal to ignite – then they're completely stuffed – and way out of their 'smaller brain' limitations (bugger me ... did I really just say that)! Nope barbecues are totally 'Men Only' territory. But hey – don't get me wrong ... women still have their uses at alfresco eating parties – like folding serviettes, keeping guests drinks topped up and looking pretty! Oh – and let's not forget the washing up of cooking utensils afterwards or the disposal of paper plates – women are really effective at that sorta thing.

And as for Christmas – well again, that's 'Bloke Territory' as due to the fact that there's always so much to do and going on at once – it really does require the 'bigger male multitasking brain' to cope. It's a fact, alas, that women would just 'crash and burn' at having to manage and juggle the cooking of the meat, all the veg and the pudding all at once. As such women are best placed to play to their strengths and just do what they're built to do best … drink sweet sherry, look pretty in a paper hat and gossip about non-present family members!

Now you might be thinking here … 'hang on there, Quaggers you complete and utter bollox spouting fuckwit … all the best cooks in the world are chefs – who are mainly men. So, Quaggers you're talking total shite … as usual'. But no … as the truth is quite simple in reality I'm afraid. I mean – men who cook are like men who perform ballet … they're raging sissys! In fact, it's a well-known fact that most male chefs (and like their 'fairy-footed' dancing friends) actually wear tights … under their ridiculous blue check patterned cooking trousers! Now before you scold me … I've actually got nothing against sissys – in fact my boyfriend is one … err scratch that last bit as actually he isn't … he's pretty butch!

But the fact of the matter and I suppose the moral of this rant is that men should do men's jobs and women, err … women's. And as such (as it wasn't a barbecue or Christmas) I shouldn't have had to have cooked my only flipping dinner!

Anyhow, as it turns out (and as I'm an adaptable male) my cooking was pretty much tip-top – and without wanting to boast – cooked to the very highest Cordon-Bleu standards. Well okay … my cucumber was a little over-done, the tomatoes toasted to buggery and the lettuce in particular was in all honesty virtually cremated. But hey … in my defence – a salad takes a lot of culinary skills to cook just right … doesn't it. Eh?

Tall Buildings on Drugs Drink Tea Out of Jugs

Do you believe in life after love? Well do you? Now this might sound (or seem, as you can't actually hear this … as its written and not spoken) like a totally random question to be asking you at the very outset of a rant. In fact, it's probably more 'randomer' <<a made up, but should be a word, word – Alert>> than a gaggle of geriatric gregarious goats eating apricot flavoured goat's cheese whilst wearing ill-fitting leopard print sombreros. But actually it's not … although to be honest, after that last sentence, I think I'd better get my backside (and the rest of me – as I don't wanna just send my ass) off to the quack's and request a bottle of 'derandomising' pills … if there is such a medication … which of course there isn't … so I won't! Eh?

So … oh hang on though … lets revert quickly, and I mean very quickly (and quicker than hot shit off a shovel) back to the reference to 'quack' … in case you're wondering, or care … or just short of something to do for a few minutes. Now a 'quack' is not just simply a duck or goose behavioural noise (do geese quack?) but instead an alternative word for the word for a doctor, whose origins stem from thousands of years ago when in ancient Latin (yup, that shite fictional language again) medical practitioners were known as 'ducktors'. And the reason for this strange moniker<<now used as slang for a name, word – Alert>>? Well this was simply due to the fact that these ducktors' primary purpose and responsibility in ancient times was focused totally on the welfare and wellbeing (same thing) of ducks … as ducks laid eggs and of course, humans … simply did not. So what you say? Well eggs and particularly those laid by 'golden ducks', err … or geese as they were … err called back then (I'm stretching this one a bit thin – I know) were the most valuable commodity in the known world … and probably in the bits that were unknown at the time as well. In fact, people's welfare was secondary back then – and if you were a duck – then you'd really made it. You were totally 'boss'. In fact, you'd be 'top duck' … which was of course the predecessor to the phrase 'top dog' as our canine best friends only came to prominence hundreds of years later when people realized (with the aid of a mirror) that backwards the word spelt 'God'!

Now alas … over the centuries both ducks and eggs fell out of popularity – which was further exasperated when gold was discovered in the wrappers of chocolate bars and eggs in boxes. And so the word used to describe a medical practitioner – for ducks gradually evolved over the years to reflect the word we now so colloquially <<awesome … but really ain't a clue what it means, word – Alert>> refer to as 'doctor'. But of course its origins will always be with our 'Anas Platyrhynchos' (you might wanna google that lil' beaut) short legged friends – aka the duck … Christ this rubbish is actually quite informative at times.

So back to my opening gambit <<odd word meaning a planned series of moves, word – Alert>> and random question asked … which seems such a very long ago time ago now. And so … do you believe in life after love?

Well that Cher woman did … and that's a G&T (I typed 'fact' there but my fingers and blinking predictive text got the better of me yet again). You know the one … she's that 18th century songstress who, with the aid of a NASA scaled plastic surgery budget, managed to keep going strong until … ooh – at least the late 1990s. Oh yeah … her flaxen-haired ladyship … must've really believed in it herself, otherwise she wouldn't have penned a global best-selling song about it. And even worse … danced around on stage wearing clothes that left little to the imagination whilst periodically bursting into strange synthetic robotic voices. You know … like the ridiculous one that is favoured by the likes of Prof Stephen Hawking. Thank God he's Mutton Jeff! I mean he must be as if he could hear himself speak – he'd have friggin changed it years ago for one that didn't sound like a drunken Dalek on heat! Now I've actually never understood why he hasn't changed it as a) he sounds like such a complete dick and surely somebody must've by now whispered this in his 'shell-like', and b) isn't he's supposed to be like cleverer than a super computer – I mean he discovered drinking establishments for birds of prey (you might need to think about that one) and of course was the inventor of Star Trek … or something like that! I think?

But hey … I've never had a problem with Cher's attire … or voice if I'm honest – and have always thought that it was fairly sexy and that she was pretty amazing for achieving so much in life without ever having the need for a surname!

So – and to get back on track – is there 'life after love?' Well I guess that depends on how you're viewing the question ... or statement, as there are at least two ways that I see it:

1. Is there life after you've lost love, i.e. can you still have a life after the love of your life has consigned <<great word that has nothing to do with prisoners' signatures, word – Alert>> you to Ditchedville – population: You?

Or,

2. Do you 'pop your clogs' after you've just 'had your oats'?

Oh, oh ... just thought of another ...

3. Do you 'pop off this mortal coil' instantaneously after you've just scored your first point in a game of tennis? Now if you're thinking that this 3rd option is stretching it a bit ... then you'd be right! If you haven't got a clue what I'm on about ... then perhaps you need to book a seat at this year's 'Wimbledon' ... or the 'US Open' ... held at the unfortunately named 'Flushing Meadows' park in New York ... which of course got its name from being located next to the world's biggest public toilets (the Meadow – that is ... and not New York). Or did it ... as honestly I ain't a clue!

Anyhow – I believe that there is life before, during and after love ... but maybe she should have changed the lyrics to refer and delve <<another word for dig, word – Alert>> into something more deep and meaningful ... and warbled ... 'Do you believe in life after death'. Eh? Now that would have got people thinking a bit deeper wouldn't it? Hey, that reminds me that I once went out with a girl who had one of her breasts made out of Oak. I said to her ... "I bet that'd be hard to squeeze ... wooden tit!" Err ...? Oh – and as for life after death or reincarnation ... now although you might scoff at the

167

idea that it actually happens, reincarnation is becoming more and more popular these days ... in fact ... it's making a comeback (groan).

Now quickly back to Cher ... before you lose the will to live. I mean what did the silicone-loving warbler actually distribute in fair and equitable portions to warrant her name? And what made her incorrectly spell it – as the words 'share' and not blinking 'Cher'? And to whom did she do this too and why? Was she trying to create a holier than though' image as an exceedingly good girl and earn 'Brownie points' in case that reincarnation thing really worked and she feared she'd come back as an Aardvark with myrmecophobia (you might also wanna Google that one too). Oh, and why did she think it was 'hip and cool' to prance about and sit astride the main deck guns of battleships (maybe Google 'image' that one ... or maybe not) donning a 'Barnet' (hair) like freaking Medusa – on a bad duvet day! Not that I'm an expert on hair mind – as the limits of that personal field of expertise these days extends no further than my bloody groin (it's not actually bloody by the way, in case you're wondering ... well only sometimes after I get clumsy during its bi-annual trim).

Err ... oh yeah – and what the frigging heck was that Sonny and Cher nonsense all about ... Eh? I mean she not only crooned with this Sonny bloke but actually thought it'd be a great idea to 'tie the knot' with him. Now I'm no marriage guidance councillor or dating agency executive ... but even I know that singers in bands should never marry one another. I mean look at Abba – they were all 'at it' and are they still experiencing a happy 'together forever' union of matrimonial bliss ... are they fuck. That bloody nonsense didn't even outlive the shelf-life of the friggin band … who crashed and burned after a few minor hits in the late '70s. Mind you, when I scoff – and perhaps somewhat unfairly – at their success … I do acknowledge that these blonde-haired beauties (except the ridiculous 'odd-one-out' ginger minger) did have some limited success. I mean at one point they were even making more profits than their country's most famous exporter 'SAAB' (Swede's Are Absolutely Brilliant) company – who were of course responsible for making Sweden's world-famous national vegetable export (maybe). Nope – in my humble, but informed opinion – she should never ever have married a man who was named after the lead singer of U2 who themselves were named after a German submarine!

So (and thankfully) finally … do you believe in life after love? Well I do … and as such I'm off the bathroom right now to 'shake hands with the unemployed', with a 'jazz mag' and a box of double ply cushion-soft tissues … and will no doubt be back in about 2 minutes' time, still breathing (albeit heavily), red faced and with a smile on my face! What! (;0)

Trousers and Pumps Clarify
Ambiguous Frumps?

1, 2, 3, 4, 5 ... or to put it another way ... One, Two, Three, Four, Five. Or to put it even another way ... the frankly, ridiculous 'Un, Deux, Trois, Quatre, Cinq'. Oh and lest <<cute little word simply meaning ... actually I'm not sure, word – Alert>> we forget the slightly less ridiculous, but even equally bizarre – Eins, Zwei, Drei, Vier, Funf.

Now on the face of it – this sounds like a pretty auspicious <<rarely used and hard to spell word, word – Alert>> start ... and "Nothing exciting here for me to literarily feast on this week, Quaggers, as it's just stupid boring numbers – or words for numbers ..." I hear you sigh!

Well ... if you can actually hear someone sigh ... I mean dies ('does' even) sighing even make a noise. Eh ... well does it? I mean, as you know – I'm a cheery fool and as such I'm not prone to sighing. So maybe you're thinking right this very second (or in a minute or two if you're having a slow day ... or have nipped out to the kitchen for a piece of cake) that I'm not remotely qualified to investigate the ability of someone to hear an emotion like sighing. Well you'd be right ... but I'm gonna go ahead and do it anyhow ... 'cos I'm annoying little fucker. Now sighing does Normandy (typed 'normally' there – but a sudden sneeze got the better of me) involve a shrugging of the shoulders, a raising of the eyebrows and importantly – an exhalation of breath. Oh, excuse me for a mo' … I'm still sneezing and on my fourth one now and I believe it's 'cos I just took my undies off – as the 'freedom of movement' lubricates my creative writing juices. Mind you what I'm doing typing in my underwear in the first place and why taking them off would cause a sternutation (shite Latin word for sneeze) is probably way too much information … so please simply forget I typed that last bit! Oh, but mind you it could be because the removal of my 'knickers' caused the setting free of my 'undergarment moths of inactivity' (married for 25+ yrs.) which made my nostrils twitchy-itchy! I kid you not as these moths grow and multiply over the years and some of them are now the size of a small dog. These don't bother me all the time though as they only flare up every 4 weeks or so … I call it my 'time of the moth' (groan)!

Err … and so back to sighing. Now whilst some expressions, like frowning or smiling can easily be executed covertly <<love that espionage type word, word – Alert>> without breaking the silence … alas, the action of pushing air from the lungs, through the diaphragm (chest) and out through the nostrils (nose) and mouth (err – mouth) can simply not be performed without making a noise. Oh no. Now whilst, albeit it, a quiet behavioural expression and certainly not one that's ever going to cause any acoustic dilemmas or fall foul of the noise abatement society – sighing actually can be heard. But hey, not if you're partially 'Mutton-Geoff' like me, or a mile away from said sigher!

Anyhow, before I disappear up a hill and come down a mountain (Google plum-voiced posh Brit actor Hugh

Grant's movies and replace the words 'I disappear' with the words 'the Englishman who went' ... and 'and come' with 'but came' ... Eh?) I'd better get back to this week's pants-rant, which of course is all about numbers.

Now at the very outset of this week's diatribe, I referred to the likes of that 'Un, Deux' and 'Eins, Zwei' as nonsense. Well, it's true – it is total rubbish. I mean what total lazy frauds those Frogs (French) and Huns (German) sorts were and how lacking in creative though they must've been when they invented their systems for counting stuff. I mean, okay, so they go and invent silly words for numbers like 'Cinq' (named after what you've done if your lying on the bottom of a swimming pool) and 'Drei' (named after what you do to yourself when you get out of the water), but then stop right there and just simply copy the English symbols for numbers ... e.g. '1' and '2' and the likes. Pathetic! I mean at least those skirt wearing nutters the Romans had the common courtesy and sense to come up with their own numeric symbols ... even if it was complete and utter ridiculous bollox ... but I'll cover that and them Latin fools later!

So right now you might be thinking – 'hey ... hang about there one god-dammed minute ... the English didn't invent numbers – it was of course someone else like ... err the Chinese'. Well, no. And although our clever oriental friends can lay claim to some of history's notable inventions like posh tea cups and saucers, the name for where farmers from Ireland grow their crops (think about it), ridiculously oversized-garden walls and rubbishy boats (really think about it) they certainly didn't invent numbers. Nope, it was indeed the English. Now please don't think that I'm being all patriotic here as remember – I'm not English or indeed British – I'm Manx. But it is a fact, that it's a little known fact

172

(although the detail is a little sketchy as I'm still making it up) that numbers were invented by the English and more specifically by an English gentlemen called Arthur Pound who lived in Tenby (albeit Wales as I'm struggling to think of an English town with a numerical name) and whose appreciative townsfolk named their town in honour of the tenth number he invented ... and simply added 'by' to the end to make it ... err, longer?

Now you might think I'm stretching the credibility fabric pretty thin here but surely if the Chinese had invented numbers then how come we've got the word 'number' for number and not something like 'ying-fu' or even '号码'? Nope – it's just plain old 'number' ... so there ... I'm right! Oh and don't even think about mentioning the Japanese as they just fell into the Franco-Germanic laziness trap and simply copied the Chinese ... and added a few different silly horizontal and vertical wiggly bits!

Nope – it was good old Arthur Pound who invented numbers 2,000 years ago or more (or less) whilst he was sitting in his cave in ancient Britain and in his bearskin trying to count his money (he also invented money which took his surname) using the then only method for adding up – sheep. Yup, in those days before numbers were invented – ancient folk used to have to count everything using sheep ... which was as confusing as fuck if you lost your place as 1 sheep was the same word as 10 of the woolly buggers. Now if you reckon that's a load of bollox (which it just might be), remember – people still count sheep today to go to sleep! Anyhow, poor old Art (as he liked to be known) did lose his place whilst counting his dosh and in frustration he had a brainwave to count all his stone coins by giving them a name and a symbol. So off he started and drew a little straight line in the clay floor of his cave and thought to himself – 'that looks like the number one!' … err … and err … that's honestly and definitely how numbers came to be (maybe). Now amongst the myriad <<great word, word – Alert>> of 'little know facts' in this week's rant – lurks (alas) another two! Firstly – old Art had a brother who was a total clueless dipstick. His name (it's important to note here that all 'same family' members in ancient times had identical first names rather than surnames – honest) was Arthur Brain and he never invented anything. Well how could he? And of course there was his cousin Arthur Dollar who emigrated to ancient America and invented money there! Now whilst this again is a little known fact – a massive tribute was actually paid to him in more recent times when US Rapper Fred Shuttlethwaite changed his name to honour him and started calling himself 50 Cent – which of course is … half a dollar! Eh?

And so – where was I … oh yes (or no – as I ain't a clue if I'm honest) well, what if numbers weren't really numbers – but instead, letters! Yes – and as crazy as that might sound (well to any normal person who isn't a skirt-wearing-feather-on-top-helmet-headed-Latin-speaking twonk … aka – a Roman) … it's actually a fact. Oh but before I go on to explore (and I will) the ridiculous use of letters for numbers … I'd better swiftly revert back to those crazy French words for numbers … as they're even shittier than Latin, in fact they really are so incredibly shite!

And so – did you hear about the French and the English cats who had a race to swim the English Channel. Now oddly and coincidentally enough they were called 'One, Two, Three, Four, Five' (the English moggy) and 'Un, Deux, Trois, Quatre, Cinq' (the

Froggy-moggy). So – who won? Well it's was 'One, Two, Three, Four, Five' of course (mega imminent groan alert) as unfortunately 'Un, Deux, Trois, Quatre … Cinq'! Now if I need to expand on that funny – then you're gonna need to … err … read more of my bollox … or learn French!

So – and thankfully back from a big diversion … it's time, as promised a long, long time ago, oh and just at the start of the previous but one paragraph – (if you're counting, or paying attention), where I revisit the crazy conundrum <<odd word that a lot of folk don't know what it means – including me, word – Alert>> … of those ridiculous Roman numerals.

Now although they demonstrated creativity and imagination, these 'bottom pinching and liquidized (and pre-liquidized) grape munchers' nearly made the mad-assed French look relatively sane – or Seine (groan … if you get this latest attempt at a gag … or simply don't if you err don't). I mean which clueless skirt wearing ancient Italian (I'll run out of phrases for Romans soon – I promise) thought up that pearl of a gem? What a complete dick they must've been … unless of course they did it unwittingly as they were totally pissed (on the squished fermented grapes), or on the other hand they were just taking the piss and having a belly laugh at everyone's else's expense. Now when I said 'on the other hand' just then it didn't really matter which one – unless you've only got one, and likewise (but in reality not) when I referred to taking the piss I wasn't meaning literally as urine ain't fun to carry about – well unless it's in your bladder! But … and here's the 'kick in the bum' for you … I am gonna go back to 'belly laugh' … albeit swiftly. Now although a common enough phrase, this really is quite impossible as tummies don't usually have mouths. Unless of course your belly button (which it actually isn't – a 'button' ... try fastening your coat with it and you'll see I'm right on this one) is actually a very small mouthpiece (it ain't). Now although my belly quite often moans and grumbles ... it ain't speaking ... it's only the voices in my head that do that. Eh!

So anyhow – and back to those blooming Roman's letters for freaking numbers? WTF ... and no, not 'World Tree Foundation'. Well they're just complete freaking nonsense – and even more so than this ... err ... freaking nonsense. I mean look at the evidence. So okay 'I' was '1' ... and fair enough – that passes the common sense 'smell test'. But then you get to 'II' for '2' and 'III' for '3'. Now you can start to see here that this is in danger of coming ridiculously tedious. And not content with just going on and on an adding the letter 'I' for each increasing number – those crazy toga wearing tosspots then went on to think it big and clever to add into the mix other friggin totally random letters!

I mean look at this lot of compete meaningless and laughable rubbish – 'L' 'C' 'D' 'M' 'X' 'V', or '50', '100', '500', '1,000', '10' and '5'. What happened to 'A'? I mean that's the first letter of the alphabet and surely should've warranted being the – err – letter for number 1. And where's 'B' and 'P' and 'F' and 'R'? There's not even an 'O' or an 'S' ... I mean at least they look at bit like the proper numbers '0' and '5'. Oh and don't even look at LXXXVIII ... although it looks like the rating of the steamiest porno flick ever ... it simply stands for the number 88? Complete cobblers! Nope these Latinos were simply at best having a massive 'Turkish' or at worst totally clueless. Is it any wonder that they're name is very nearly (ish) an anagram for moron ... nearly.

Anyway – enough of this numerical claptrap, as I'm actually starting to feel a bit frisky now as numbers do in fact really turn me on. Oh yes – and as such I'm gonna have to sign off right now and go and indulge in a bit of that age old traditional man and woman thing … better known as a LXIX.

Svelte Badgers and Stoats Feign Pelican Votes!

I'll bet those 'so-called' (we'll come back to that little 'ditty' a bit later) Commonwealth Games athletes are so incredibly pissed off right now.

I mean ... come on Commonwealth Games Committee ... get your bloody act together and show the 'Athletes' at least a modicum of compassion. So – what am I blooming getting at I hear you muse? Well it's simply this. These so-called sporty (not spotty – mind ... although some of them are) types 'train' all their lives in order that they can attend these (ahem) 'sporting events' – with the sole driving reason being so they can enjoy an exotic trip to some far away sunny, hot country to (ahem) compete.

So – after spending their whole lives and spare time running around, jumping over things, riding bikes and throwing stuff ... which tropical sun-kissed paradise do the fruits of all their hard work – reward them with? The Bahamas, Fiji, the Maldives ... Tahiti? No. Oh frigging no. The poor sods have ended up in frigging Glasgow. Not Glasgow Australia (if there is one) ... or even Glasgow Island in the Caribbean (there isn't one) ... but freaking Glasgow Scotland. Yes, fucking Scotland.

Now which bright freaking spark thought that it was a good idea to send people (who've stupidly given up all their spare time on the enticement of – a 'paid by nation' free holiday to some hot country) to bloody Scotland? Now don't get me wrong – I'm not anti-scots or anything like that – it's just that basically – Scotland's a freaking toilet. Now before you get all uppity with me in defence of 'Jock-Land' … let's examine the facts.

Well it's always raining in Scotland – unless it's snowing and to cope with this shite hand Mother Nature has dealt them – they're all complete alcoholics. Really. Yes – indeed – it's a fact that all Scots drink whisky for water and they even use it to clean their teeth with and wash their privates with. Have you ever smelled a Scotsman's privates? No … well I have – up really close – and they stank of a 12yr old Malt. Ooh – hang on – what was I doing sniffing a Scotsman's 'meat and two veg' … err well that's for another day and if I'm totally honest – I wished I hadn't typed that bit now. But hey, once typed its typed and I can't use correction fluid on my iPad can I. Oh – hang on there, though, one dang minute <<super thought alert>> – I might just write to the big boss – 'Mr A Pple' (his ancestors had a stutter) and give him a top money making idea to develop and include a 'correction' or 'delete text' button for the iPad/iPhone. I'd certainly download that App – and would even pay for it (max 69pence though) – as I'm always sending emails and texts that are absolutely littered with typos and things I wish I could've corrected or deleted!

So back to bloody Scotland. Well … as well has having absolutely shite fucking weather – the country is populated mainly by red-headed transvestite men called Jimmy. Oh yeah … all the men wear flipping checked skirts with weird furry purses slung around their waists – just in front of their willies. And they don't wear and blooming knickers either. Not because they're hardy types – oh no- it's just so they can flash they're ginger hair covered bits whilst going up escalators or doing handstands – which they do all the time (err … I'll bet)!

And additionally – and really worryingly so – don't ever, ever bring your swimming costume to Scotland – as you won't be able to friggin use it.

Oh no … be very fucking careful – if you're ever thinking about taking a dip in any Scottish rivers or lakes. Don't do it. All the waterways in Scotland are full of big necked prehistoric monsters … with sharp teeth and flippers! They might be shy – and only show themselves every 50 years or so – but they're there believe me – I've seen one … well – albeit once and in my sleep!

Now don't get me wrong – I'm not 'Scottist' <<new made up, word – alert>> and anti-Scottish. Oh no, in fact Scotland is one of my favourite places in the whole wide world to visit … well, it's in the top 900 (just), but really – what a dull fecking place it is!

And so – those poor-poor foolish gullible individuals must really feel like right twats now as the Scottish mist and rain greets them. I'll bet! BTW, <<abbreviation alert>> I mentioned the shite weather … well Scotland has just the two types of climate and as such – it's either a) raining, or B) about to rain!

Anyhow – I referred at the very start of this meaningless ramble that the Commonwealth Games are a so called 'sporting event'. It might sound like I'm devaluing them or at the very least 'scoffing' <<a Quaggers' favourite, word – alert>> about their worth. Well … … okay, I am. I mean, come on … half the blooming world ain't competing at them – so at best they're simply a poor-man's Olympics. I could blooming win them … I'm sure – especially the ladies' events … give us a pink leotard and a wig … and I'd have a bloody go!

Indeed! Now these deluded fools might think they're world beaters … but they're not really, they're just mucking about! I should know … I myself am a well-honed athlete … the evidence is clear. I'm great at darts, snooker, pool and a dab hand at chess. So when it comes to talking sport – you're looking at numero one!

So let's quickly look at the evidence of a few of these … so-called 'sports' and err … 'athletes'.

Swimming: These feckers spend their whole lives getting up really early in the morning to train. Why? Once you can swim – you can bloody swim … you don't need to bleeding arse-about training early every morning. I mean, if you love water so blooming much you can just go to a public swimming pool at weekends or take a deep bath wearing your trunks.

Cycling: These Lycra clad morons are just having a kinky laugh. Cycling isn't a bleeding sport it's a pastime!

The marathon: What is the bloody point in half killing yourself running 26 freaking miles … when you could just take a cab. This is the 21st Century guys … we've got motor powered devices nowadays?

The javelin: What's up with just playing darts down the pub … and you stay dry if it's wet and can enjoy a beer and a packet of peanuts. A much better use of your time.

The long jump: What a load of childish nonsense that is. "Will You Bloody Grow Up Guys!?" … I yell at the TV when that's on. I mean, I stopped jumping into sandpits when I was about frigging 5 years old!

Finally (and I could go on believe me) …

Gymnastics: This is just a complete waste of energy … and a bit weird if you ask me. I mean it's more people in Lycra – but this time 'poncing' about like fairies. I don't know if you're like me – but don't you just wanna see 'em trip over or even better – fall off some apparatus or equipment! Don't you!

And so – that's enough of this ranting for now as I'm starting to get peckish and I've got a bowl of my favourite 'Scotch eggs' that are imminently about to meet their maker … and I don't mean the chef from the factory where they were manufactured! Oh – and one quick very final thought … Scotch eggs – is that where every Scottish person comes from?

Those Impractical Propensities of Untrained Aberrant Seas?

So ... by now you're probably wondering what the deck ('heck' even) is this nonsense all about! Or you might've fallen asleep, or worse still – died of boredom akin to that of watching wood warp ... or metal rust! Oh hang on though (not literally mind as – what too and why?) ... you aren't of course bored, be-baffled <<just made it up word – Alert>>, or bemused yet as this is only the start of this latest serving of complete bollox! The boredom will come soon ... be patient!

So without further ado <<doesn't look right but is an actual word – Alert>>, I'm actually for once gonna cut to the chase (is there one and what does that mean?) and talk about 'cheese' – as I promised in some far distant rant a while ago ... no really I did.

So, 'cheese'. Erm ... you know what ... I'm actually gonna change my mind (I bet you wish I would and go and get one that works) ... and I'm instead gonna (groan) go back to that 'cutting to the chase' comment as I just couldn't let that little ditty go without further investigation (groan II). Now before you have a go at me ... and to be fair ... a man has every right to change his mind as it's not just a woman's prerogative <<ain't used that word in a while ... and had trouble spelling it – Alert>> to do so. Now not literally 'change my mind' as that would be frankly ridiculous, impractical and nigh on impossible. I mean you'd have to cut open a trap door in the top of your head and then extrapolate <<wow – aren't I an intellectual, word – Alert>> the part of the brain that is your mind and free it from all the connecting bits and bobs … you know the wires and cables that hold it in place and make it do stuff … like think. That said, and however difficult it would be to actually remove your mind, how would you know which bit of your brain was indeed your 'mind'? I mean – is it all of it … or just a part of it … and is it labelled 'MIND'?

Oh and you'd need a big full length mirror to see what you were doing as you were removing your Mind (like in clothes shops) and a big pair of scissors and a shoe horn <<not a musical instrument – but completely something else word – Alert>>!

Now before we go on – I need to go back to those flipping full length mirrors in clothes shops. Why don't they just replace them with big TV screens with a really fit and hot male or female model on screen wearing what you were trying on … err, but not full length enough to get the head in as then you'd know it wasn't you … err! Then when you'd stand in front of it wearing the item of clothing you were trying on … you'd think … 'Wow, I look great in this – it really fits like a glove' (only it wouldn't – unless you were actually buying gloves) … and you'd buy it. I mean – why is it that clothes always look better on the pics of models in the shops, or on those peculiarly <<thought you know how to spell … but don't, word – Alert>> named mannequins (are there womannequins?) … and then when you get 'em home … you look like a sack of potatoes that a horse with a bladder infection has just urinated on! Well that happens to me … anyhow! Mind you they'd have to make sure that they had the correct sex of model programmed into the 'clothes tryer-on-erer' <<made up word, word – Alert>> big TV as you wouldn't wanna stand there in a pretty summer dress and see a hairy-arsed trucker with a tattoo of a … err 'anchor'? … staring back at you! Although, thinking about it … would they have a hairy arsed trucker as a model – and do they have hairy bottoms … hmmm … I'll move on … as that's for another rant … Hmm!

Anyhow, back to the subject of 'cheese' … oh no it's that odd comment or phrase I'm actually gonna babble or talk about today … ermm OK … shit … Quaggers think of some crap to write.

Okay, so … I mean – what is it with these stupid, meaningless and (in my opinion) far too eagerly thrown about phrases that the English language has somehow seemed to have so readily adopted. "What silly phrases?" I hear you nervously ponder. Well I'm on about phrases like 'cut to the chase' and not 'cut to the cheese' though … as a) there's no such phrase and b) I'm not now talking about cheese this time … so what the fooking hell's that phrase all about. Eh?

I mean 'cutting to the chase'! What are we chasing and what are we cutting … oh – and with what? Its complete bollox!

And there's loads of these erroneous <<clever and – do I really know what that word means – Alert>>, phrases, so let's look at a few examples:

'That's the straw that broke the camel's back!' WTF … some fooking strong straw that … and wouldn't its hump (full of water) prevent its back from breaking …

acting like a sort of 'airbag' … but one filled with water (a waterbag)?

And on that theme … 'That's the final straw!' What is and why … and who cares?!? If you run out of straws, then just drink it straight from the glass or bottle. It's hardly the end of the world! Or you could fashion one from an old toilet roll cardboard tube … no hang on … scratch that idea as it would be too wide and as such hard to suck … and it would get soggy … so best not. Hmm!

Then there's such ridiculous sayings, like – 'keen as mustard!' Is it … and why?

And 'cool as a cucumber!' I mean how cool can one of those be? Now if it was wearing a 'SuperDry' ('Made in Japan' – yeah we know) jacket and a pair of stonewashed Levi's Jeans, and silver-tipped cowboy boots … then perhaps. But without that apparel <<another word for clothes – Alert>> how cool can a cucumber really be?

Then there's 'pie in the sky' – when scoffing an idea? Has anyone ever seen bits of pie floating in the clouds? Maybe you could then scoff them and not the idea?

What about – 'drunk as a skunk'! Ever seen one? Neither have I … let alone one that was 'pissed as a newt' … oh and there's another daft as a brush (are they?) phrase. A really small frog-like animal consumed by alcohol – I mean – c'mon … really!

Well there's loads of these feckers – but I'll end on two equine <<posh word for a horse – Alert>> themed ones, like … 'straight from the horse's mouth!' So what is … and why does this mean that's it's a sorta factual fact from the originator? I mean horses can't friggin speak (okay – Mr Ed could – but was he real)? I mean – never mind having the ability to bleeding well talk … have you ever seen a horse even trying to chew a mint … its mouth is all over the friggin place … loose and clumsy … like Bambi on ice! No way could it ever form words! Neigh! Sorry!

And finally (finally) – 'don't look a gift horse in the mouth!' What the fook's that all about? Why would you want to look at a horse's mouth … unless you were either a horse dentist or giving it a mint? And why would it be a gift horse? I mean what gifts has anyone ever received from a horse … apart from manure when you've had the misfortune of following along a road or path that one has recently trotted upon. It's not like the tooth fairy or even that Father Christmas is a horse … and bears gifts. Father Christmas isn't a horse by the way. No, he's a reindeer dressed as an old age pensioner! Err …?

Anyhow … and that all said – there is actually one crazy saying that I know the origins of – and remarkably it is the one (and only one to my knowledge … which admittedly ain't great) that makes sense – when you know the know. And so – I'm actually gonna talk some reverse bollox for once and tell you so stink (meant to type 'something' there – but wearing boxing gloves as I type this)? That, a) is correct and b) is something you didn't know you didn't know.

Oh – but before I do – I gotta quickly swipe back to boxing gloves as you're no doubt wondering why I'm wearing them right now?

Well (and with me possibly teetering on the brink of Too-Much-Information's-Ville … population Me), I'm lying on the bed typing this rubbish – and basically old habits die hard. You see I was very excitable and fidgety … and adventurous as a boy and as such (and to enable me to get some sleep at night) my Mum and Dad used to make me wear boxing gloves in bed! I'll let you join the dots there … No – really – I'm only joking – although it would be hard to you know what with boxing gloves on! Err … moving ever so swiftly on.

And so back to the minuscule and tiny <<mean the same so I've just wasted a word – Alert>> fragment of wisdom I'm gonna share with you that isn't complete and utter claptrap <<not a word meaning a means for getting rid of an STD – Alert>>. So … here it is – the phase 'back to square one'. Well this everyday phrase has its origins in sports commentary on the radio – before the TV was in every household. The sport was football (soccer) and commentators would basically break the pitch up into squares to help explain to the listeners where the ball was. So when the ball was back into the goalkeeper's hands ready to start play again – they called this area the '1st square of pitch – or square one. And so – we're back to square one … which of course we're not luckily for you as I'm just about to run out of finger ink … and will stop typing very soon!

Like now…!

Artisan Blokes Sweating Pink Turtle Artichokes!

Ooh, I tell you what, I've been so very, very excited this week (or last week, a few weeks/ months ago if it's not late May as you're reading this). So excited in fact, that I peed my pants on at least several occasions ... and not just little indiscreet leaks – oh no ... a blooming deluge. It was like the Niagara Falls down there in 'Meat and Two Veg Land' and akin to a veritable <<love that word but don't use it that often, word – Alert>> biblical flood. In fact, there was so much water sloshing around in my knickers that at one stage I actually did contemplate rushing off into the garden shed – grabbing a hammer, nails and wood, and constructing a miniature Ark for my 'wrinkly walnut danglers' and 'soul pole'. In the end I didn't – but I tell you what – I hope the wife doesn't check her 'panty-liner' drawer any time soon!

Oh – and before you cry ... "Ooh what a pervert, wearing his wife's 'downstairs' protection stuff!" ... I'm actually not, I was just trying to be practical and prevent trouser-staining seepage. And I'll have you know ... it's actually quite difficult to make an effective water retention or damp proofing device for the male gusset or 'wedding gear' out of panty-liners ... as let's face it ... our groin a freaking ridiculous shape. This is probably why I went through a pack of 12 and half a roll of

Sellotape. Still, it was a 'two for the price of one' value pack of 'female flange flaps' ('FFFs'), so I hope the 'trouble and strife' won't mind that much when she discovers that my over-excitement driven flood prevention activities have robbed her of next month's supply of 'crabby-cycle-clitoris-covers' ('CCCCs')! Oh how I so love these acronyms, although the 1st looks like it stands for some sort of militia and the latter – the former name for the Soviet Union!

To put it another way (and hey – one that doesn't involve 'toilet' talk), this week I've been more excited than a giraffe wearing luminous green latex leggings on its way to an all you can eat and drink ceiling-painting party … possessing an entry pass that states – *'This Ticket Entitles the Bearer to Fill Their Face for Free – Provided You've Got a Spotty 7ft High Neck'.*

"So why has this deranged Viking simpleton been all giddy and expectant this week?" I here (oops 'hear') you ponder …

"Has he just discovered that properly functioning brain transplants without the renegade DUF ('dumb as fuck') chromosome, are now available free of charge for complete and certifiable idiots?"

Or …

"Has he just been told that you can now buy pet dust – and he's about to buy his very own pedigree 'dust pet' this weekend so he can pamper it and take it out for dust walks?"

Or …

"Has he just learned to tell the time on his day-glow plastic Disney character watch after finally working out that Mickey's hands were actually pointing to numbers and not waving to him?"

Well no, and ponder ye not anymore … 'cos finally – and after wasting 3 odd paragraphs on utter unadulterated porcupine poo – I'm actually gonna 'spill the beans'. Not literally mind, as we had peas for tea, and anyhow beans are actually quite hard to spill as they'd sorta just slide very, very slowly from the plate in the thick, gloopy (and rather delicious if you don't mind) tomato ketchup sauce which slows the rate of slippage down quite a lot. BTW – I once tried to measure the length of time that it took a solitary baked bean (Heinz of course – as other brands aren't worth a wank on a wet-weekend) to slide off a plate – tilted to 45 degrees. Well, all I can say is don't fucking try it – that's my advice to you. I was still waiting for some 'bean' action 24 hours later and can conclude that the rate of slippage was slower than an elderly snail with a wooden leg riding a bicycle with square wheels up a steep hill! Another conclusion I arrived at is that baked beans are only good for one thing – and that's for allowing you to possess the gift of being able to orchestrate the most amazing bottom burps … shortly after consuming a plate full. Incidentally, mine, after eating a whole tin, can be heard nearly a mile away and smelt for 2 miles (5 if downwind). It's actually true to say – and I'm not proud of this – but after eating a 500g tin of baked beans I emit a putrid stench for a whole 2 days and one so powerful it's been known to close public buildings I've been visiting. Basically it's a smell like something has crawled up inside my ass – taken up residence there … and then a slow and horrible death!

And so … and frigging-well finally I hear you groan – what's going on in my microscopic mind and little world to get me all in an excitable 'frothing at the mouth' (not a good look, but I always carry a handkerchief for just such an occasion) frenzy? Well, quite simply ... my tiny island is now (yes now) under invasion.

Oh yeah ... I'll say that again in caps for effect/affect (I can never work out that one) – OH YEAH!

Now we're not being invaded by Vikings as they'd be like way too old by now (its 1,000 years+ since they landed) to even get off the beach let alone pose any kinda threat to our island's sovereignty and independence. I mean they'd like need – Viking walking sticks or Viking wheel chairs and would struggle to make any headway up the coarse shingle and sand that adorns our islands beaches. And anyhow, I can only imagine it'd be dam hard to wield a battle axe and sword whilst leaning on a walking stick ... or plonked in a moving chair. I mean an 'attack wheelchair's' manoeuvrability would prove problematic as the steps to ascend the island's promenades from the shore are not very 'elderly warrior' access friendly. No. Alas they were mainly built in the Victorian days when all they cared about was building stuff that would only work if powered by steam ... and wearing tall hats! Actually and thinking about it – they were pretty odd those Victorians with all their steam shenanigans <<awesome word, word – Alert>> instead of simply using electricity ... but hey, they must've impressed the Queen of England at the time though as she even changed her name to theirs. Hang on though?

Anyway – I digress as always ... and I'm harder to keep on track than one of those supermarket shopping trolleys that has a wobbly wheel. You know, the one you just always, always get – even if there's like 100 to pick from. It's like it sits there waiting for you to arrive at the shopping mall and when it spies you with its beady shopping trolley eyes – it winks to itself and then emits into the air a plume of secret and invisible 'pick me ya dumb-ass' pheromones (like hormones but named after ancient Egyptian kings rather than 'ladies of the night') which lure you in like its prey! Embarrassed and too polite to choose another one – you struggle around the shop with the outside appearance of the patience of a saint … but whilst quietly mumbling and grumbling to yourself that "this is a complete pile of wank" – I might've mentioned the wank word twice now in this rant … uh oh, 3 times now so I will stop … honest! Oh and choosing an alternative trolley wouldn't really be an option anyhow as no matter which one you chose – 'old wonky-wheel-wanker' (oops – 4 times) would simply morph itself into the next one you bloody picked! Oh and quickly back to 'hormone' … here's a question for you. How do you make a hormone? Kick her in the cunt!

Anyhow – moving very quickly on … err, where the bloody hell was I? Oh yeah – the island's annual invasion. This amazing event happens every year and starts on the weekend at the beginning of the last week in May. Yup that'll be right now then (or not as previously mentioned). And so … and bloody finally … It's TT races time.

Yup the world famous Isle of Man Tourist Trophy motorcycle races.

Basis Ally – I actually attempted to type 'Basically' there – but big fingered syndrome got the better of me and fuggered me up! Fuggered – BTW – is the word that lets you get away with saying 'fucked' and 'buggered' without getting into trouble … back of the net! Oh and coincidentally Ally is the wife's name – spooky –

perhaps she's secretly watching me type this shite? I hope not … although to be fair – I've not actually slated the moaning old boot in this rant. Oops. Ouch!

Anyhow – and Christ I'm an absolute nightmare … if there was a tax on freaking words used – I'd be one poor fucker. I'd be broke and living in a cave with only the 3 bears for company and warm, not hot, not cold porridge to eat (plenty sugar though – and not that 'sweetener' shite)! By the way – what the fucking hell is that 'sweetener' bollox all about? I mean why invent stuff for stuff that's already there? We've had sugar since it was 1st discovered in the sugar mines of Sumatra in 1 million years BC, so why bloody tinker with it and making a friggin substitute? And anyhow … and as me old gran used to say (before she was sadly taken from us after being run over by a drunken tooth-ache troubled horny elephant on a wheel-less unicycle) … "If it was bad for you, they would never had invented it!"

Finally (it won't be BTW) – to get back on track, I was gonna say …

Basically the TT sees 50,000 bikers invade my island (although don't own it) every year for two weeks. It's an amazing specs table ('spectacle' – my typing's really shite today) and the whole island is a buzz! Roaring sounds and petrol fumes fill the island's usual melancholic air with thousands of sweaty leather clad bikers, with bulging beer guts, more facial hair than ZZ Top after being marooned on a desert island for 10 years and the stench of a skunk's armpit! Oh and the male bikers are quite gross as well.

Motorcycle riding … ooh what a thrill and what total excitement. There's nothing like having ya legs straddled across a throbbing powerful thrusting beast –

but hey – enough thinking about me as I'm actually talking about riding a blooming motorcycle.

It's truly amazing though, very, very busy, but so very amazing. If you could bottle the atmosphere of TT fortnight then you'd make a flipping fortune. Mind you – you'd need a freaking big bottle to capture it in and then a purpose built factory to facilitate the transfer of the 'atmosphere' into smaller bottles and then a robust marketing strategy to sell them … hmm – I'm thinking way too much into this.

Well that you have it – the root of my excitement and a few facts thrown in as well for good measure. And so finally, – and talking of races – I was at another type of race the other day – the four-legged type – yup Horse racing. So there I was at a horse race and I just got one of those gut feelings to put a bet on a horse called 'MyFace'. The odds were 20:1 so I put a fiver on it and thought to myself – 'hey Quaggers – you could make a hundred spondooleys (money) here.' So there I was in the crowded grandstand as the race neared its conclusion and my horse was really up for it and galloping (faster than hot shit off a shovel) towards the finishing line. Sensing a money spinning win, I excitedly started frantically shouting my horses name loudly and repeatedly, over and over again. As they neared the line I got this eerie feeling that all was not right and I noticed that the crowd had fallen silent. I looked around to see hundreds of people staring disdainfully at me and with open mouths. It was then that I started to feel really, really embarrassed and very, very awkward – as the realization hit me that I'd been screaming repeatedly, "Come on MyFace, come on MyFace … please come on MyFace!"

I shrunk away … and made a sharp exit!

And very finally I just thought I mention that TT fortnight <<what an odd word for 2 weeks, word – Alert>> lasts for – yup you've guessed it – for two whole weeks as is on now (or not)! So please feel free (or somebody else if 'free' objects) to check it out here:

www.iomtt.com/TT-Info.aspx

Enjoy … and hey, maybe come and visit next year. Amongst the amazing atmosphere and fun packed thrills … you could get to see some truly awesome places and things … like me! Err …?

Theodolite Fixtures Invert
Gingerbread Pictures?

So finally it's that monumental time when I'm actually gonna go off on one and produce a 'Pants and Rants' extraordinaire <<French sounding … that's actually – English, word – Alert>> in respect of one of my favourite foods. And so – this rant is going to be totally and udderly (you'll see what I did there in a sec …) devoted to congealed cows stomach and bladder juices – or as we like to call it … cheese!

So before I get side-tracked, like I did the other week – I'm diving straight into cheese! Not literally though … as I'd need a really big amount (a lorry load or more) of soft creamy cheese to break my dive and stop me hurting myself. Oh … and a big, big bowl to put it in … that was deep enough to … Err, dive into? And hey (as diversion danger starting to creep in) … not that blooming rubbishy 'Swiss cheese' – you know … the stuff you always see on ('in' even) cartoons like 'Tom and Jerry' – that's blooming full of holes. Yeah – holes … what the fuck is all that about! Eh? I mean, if I dived into that – knowing my 'sod's law' luck … I'd very accurately fall head first – arms outstretched – through one of the freaking holes … and bang my friggin head on the bottom of the bowl. Oh yeah – and mentioning once again 'sod's' law (whoever 'Sod' was) … I'd end up falling through a 'deliberately' made gap in the fluffy cheese. Now when I say 'deliberately' made … I'm not talking shite … which is a fist! Oops – not a 'fist', by the way, but a 'first' … the difference being a strategically placed 'r' … making all the difference between a clenched hand (or something rude) and finishing something better than second. Err – I'm starting to digress again … and so …

Yes, anyhow back to 'deliberately made'. I mean they must be … mustn't they – or how else would Swiss cheese be full of those tiny little annoying freaking holes? Now whilst you wouldn't think that it would make great business sense to make a cheese full of holes … as that would simply devalue the price per weight profit when you came to sell it (as holes don't weigh jack-shit) … those holes can't just appear by themselves. I mean surely they couldn't just happen overnight of their own volition <<Ooh look at me … Mr Clever Pants, word – Alert>> could they … you know, after the cheese maker had spent hours carefully crafting his milky mousse and had gone to bed for the night … leaving them to set … err on the window ledge (do they)? So there must be another reason as to why the cheese gets all full of holes?

Well, yes there is. Mice. Oh yes … those furry grey little whisker-faced rodents (or white in colour if they're the pet variety … or the sugar ones you buy in sweet ships … Err meant to type 'shops' there as 'sweet ships' is ridiculous … although I'll bet they are exported by sea). Anyhow – back on track Quaggers you fool. So holes being deliberately put into Swiss cheese … and mice. Well … (and prepare yourself for this as I'm going to whisk your brain off on a brief but crazy fantasy mystery tour) … there are actually Swiss hating and cheese addicted mice ... or to give them their Latin name 'Swisshateus-cheesilitious'. Now, these little critters, who are indigenous <<ooh – look at me again, word – Alert>> to Switzerland, (or anywhere else that Swiss cheese is made) just love to climb up the outside walls of the Swiss cheese maker's cheesery <<new word for a cheese maker's house – Alert>> in the dead of night as the cheeses (un-holed at this juncture) lay setting on the window ledges. And like commandos – driven on by their insatiable cravings and using sheer mouse-stealth-perfection ... they gorge themselves on their booty – lovely juicy cheese. Now (and I might've kinda forgot to mention just before) as these 'Swisshateus-cheesilitious' mice are very tiny (postage stamp sized) and have eating disorders (their appetite is very poor – akin to that of a malnourished ant on a diet) ... they don't actually obliterate <<great and powerful sounding, word - Alert>> much of the cheese. Nope they just leave little holes that they burrowed as they've pathetically gorged. And that's how Swiss cheese gets its 'deliberately' made holes!

Sounds a bit mental ... well it is 'Emmental' ... isn't it (you might wanna Google that)!

Anyhow ... isn't 'Cheese' really weird stuff, pleasant to eat and on the face of it ... harmless – but weirder than 'Weird Al Yankovic' ... (you're gonna have to google that as well)! This guy is\was (not sure if he's still with us) weirder than me ... and that's weirder than Weird Al Yankovic ... err? Anyhow ...

Weird and perhaps also not that pleasant? Well ... let's look at the evidence before us ... well that, that's <repeated word but okay to use Alert>> floating about forlornly in my tiny but barren and empty brain.

Well cheese really is vile stuff ... and should carry a government public health warning! I mean if you think about it (and maybe you shouldn't) – it's gotta contain cow's piss ... or goat's piss, if it's goat's cheese – as that only comes from a goat and not a cow apparently ... unless you've got a cross-dressing transvestite 'Cow-Goat'? (;0) Yeah – cheese must contain bovine <<clever word for a cow-like animal – Alert>> urine as milk is a liquid produced by a cow. Now a person's only body liquid – is piss (steady let's keep this clean when talking bodily fluids) so it makes sense that the same must apply to a cow. Okay – and I've gotta go back to the 'keep it clean' comment ('cos my 'mucky' mind means I just can't resist) – there are a few other bodily fluids – but let's face it – cheese ain't 'spit' or 'jizz' ... or even runny (if you've eaten a bad curry the night before) pooh ... anyhow it'd be the wrong colour ... unless it was chocolate cheese – and there's no such thing (Err ... I think).

Oh and before you even think about getting on your 'high horse' (Err – horses deserve a rant all to themselves – and that gem's to come another week) cow's milk is not the same as when ladies produce milk – as that's just for babies – and they only produce a few bottles worth of that for a couple of days after they've given birth (no, really ... I googled it). And cows produce milk every day (gallons of the stuff) and they don't have babies every day do they – as the bloody world would be overrun with bleeding cows! And it ain't ... well not quite ... although there is that place in the Isle of Wight? Therefore, what comes out of a cow must be piss and I'm afraid that's called milk and milk is what makes cheese! And so ... we've established (we have – honest) beyond scientific doubt that milk = piss and as milk = cheese (that's been shook up a bit), therefore, cheese = milk + piss. Simple!

So – when you're eating a lovely Swiss, Austrian, French or English cheese … you're really eating solidified cow's piss. Still it's nice though – especially with crackers and wine … the dry biscuity crackers actually soak up the piss somewhat don't you think?

So … and finally … and I know what's on the tip of your tongue (not cheese I'll bet anymore) … "What is that cheeky-crazy-rascal Quagger's favourite ever cheese … since he is such a fan and obviously a complete connoisseur" <<French sounding, but again an English word, word – Alert>>> "of the fatty cow bladder bi-product?" Well you're right of course – I am a lover of cheese. In fact, it will come as no surprise that I'm a bit of an expert in the field of dairy products and in particular those produced by milk being frantically shaken to produce a creamy end product like an excited man with his appendage in his grip! Erm – forget that last bit.

And so … yes … and to be honest – I am a complete, total and utter cheese snob! Indeed, only the best cheeses get to cross my lips and excite my well-educated culinary pallet!

And so … my favourite cheese … well that's simple …

Melted cheese!

Stunned Buses in Coats Marry Cross-Dressing Boats?

Okay ... and yeah – I know what you're thinking ... no, actually I do.

Now I'm not gonna go over all that ... 'I can actually hear you' tripe like I did previously (or in the future?) ... 'cos I know that that (Sstutter alert) really did your noggin in. Oh and if you're not sure what a noggin is – well then you're actually gonna learn something from me today! No really – these rants of mine ain't just always filled up with the top to toe bullshit. No way Jose!

Now wait right there ... if we're gonna go down the road of 'Mexicanizms' ... ('Jose's' the Mexican name for a hose) then ... what the freaking hell is 'Mexico City' all about. I mean really ... what's all that about? Now excuse me if I'm being a tad harsh here – but how incredibly unimaginative are Mexicans ... eh? I mean what sort of an incredibly lame-brained excuse for a name for your capital city is that ... and I wonder how much thought actually went into arriving at that little gem?

Now you can just picture the very first ever two Mexicans sat around a table (shaped like a fajita) whilst drinking tequila and debating ...

1st born Mexican 'Jose':

"Hic … whatz shaz wez callz ours capitalz zity whenz wez buildz itz?"

2nd born Mexican 'Jose B':

"Gringo – isz don'tz knowz!"

Hey and hang on a mo' … have you ever noticed (and I just have as I was writing this) how many 'Zs' there are in the Mexican official language 'Mexicanianz'? Bloody hundreds of them, that's how many – they love 'em. I mean look at their very 1st ever president – he was called 'Zorro'!' Even their national animal is a zebra … (although I mighta made that last bit up … and the bit before … and the bit before that). Oh … and I bet you didn't know that my wide range of languages extended to a fluent understanding of Mexicanianz – did you? Err … well okay – it doesn't and I'm actually only fluent in English (well nearly) and Gibberish!

Anyhow … so after hours of getting sloshed and a siesta or two thrown in for good luck, these very first two ever Mexican 'pillocks of the community' drew a complete blank and simply put the two words they were thinking about together … Mexico (which is Mexicanianz for Mexico … erm) and City (which is Mexicanianz for a town with more than 3 tequila bars. And so 'Mexico City' was born … although in Mexicanianz it's actually pronounced 'Mexicoz Zity' (didn't know that now did ya)! Anyway – come on Mexico … get you're thinking caps on and why don't you come up with a name for your capital city that has a bit of thought behind it … it's not too late!

What about 'Sombrerosville' or even 'Wave' – named after their favourite national sport … they all do

203

it ... and are actually quite good at it as well (even though, in reality ... it's just waving in groups like demented lemmings)!

Mind you those Mexicans are not alone in their complete lack of imagination when it comes to the naming of their capital cities. I mean look at Brazil – 'Brasilia' (okay they did something the Mexicans would never do and drop a 'Z') and what about Panama? How despairingly unimaginative were they. I mean, they named their capital city after a freaking canal. They even named they're country after it. Wow ... how completely thoughtless!

And then there's 'Rome'. Now they might've conquered half the world but them girly-skirt-wearing troublemakers utilized not one ounce of their 'grey matter' and simply named their capital city after their capital city! Err – oh hang about though. And them the Italians, who were obviously too busy eating silly-stringy-bland food and pinching ladies' bottoms, came along and very lazily just stole their capital city name off the Romans – who by that time had inexplicably all buggered off to live in Turkey!

Hey and don't even mention Nicaragua who named theirs after a bloke from the country (google it) ... and what about bloody Cuba – who just named their capital after a blooming fat cigar! Bonkers or what?

At least the French (they had to be good for something – I suppose) put a wee bit of thought into it and named their capital after some ancient Trojan guy in a skirt ... on a horse.

Even supposedly über-clever religious people are susceptible <<infrequently used word, word – Alert>> to 'lack of imagination' moments, as well. I shit you not. I mean ... 'The Vatican City' ... come on guys, for fuxsake ... put some bloody thought into it ... your country is called the 'Vatican City' – so can't you at least come up with a different name for your capital ... eh?

Oh and what about Canada ... well I suppose they at least showed some imagination and named their capital city after their furry little water loving national animal ... and simply spelt it wrong (you might have to google that as well ... and if so perhaps you'd better plonk an atlas on your Christmas List). But hey, the prize goes to those crazy Aussies – who thought it would be a great idea to name their capital after their national pastime – drinking tinnies of beer. No, really. Years later they then had a change of heart to try to gain international credibility and to try to disguise the fact that the country was in reality just a very big deserted field with a red stone in the centre of it and populated by blokes called 'Bruce' wearing silly hats with corks in, quaffing (I love that word) lager! Yup – so they simply jumbled the words up to now spell Canberra!

Then there's blooming India (a massive country with little imagination) who named their capital after a shop selling fancy food. And what about South Korea's – named after the bottom of a shoe! At least they weren't as clueless as their cousins up there in North Korea who simply took the load of unused letters from a game of Scrabble and hey presto – Pyongyang (word score about 34).

Finally on this theme ... you're probably thinking to yourself – 'so that Quaggers is sitting there slagging off other nation's lack of imagination in the naming of their capital cities – when his is just named after some random bloke'. Well, and as me old dad used to say – "It's not often you're right ... but you're wrong this time!" Indeed – 'Douglas' (that's my capital's name) is actually named not after a guy called Douglas, but after the place where two rivers meet – the river 'Dhoo' and the river 'Glass'. Basically my Viking ancestors just then simply glued the two bits together ... in between bouts of sailing silly shaped boats, pillaging and eating raw fish.

So finally ... where was I? Oh yeah ... I was gonna explain 'noggin'. Well 'noggin' is a word we use for your head. Now I'm talking about the one on your shoulders by the way – you know – the one your hair resides on (not in my case) ... and not the other one that adorns your genitalia (if you're a bloke) and dangles precariously and somewhat ridiculously between a man's legs. Nope – a 'noggin' is a person's bonce ... or head.

So there you go and please put that one in your 'Things I've Learnt from Pants Rants' book – erm page 1, first and last entry!

Anyhow, I'm gonna have to end this ramble now as the grass won't cut itself! Hey though – imagine if it could ... how much work would that save, eh! Mind you you'd have to be careful not upset it though as it might then refuse to keep itself trim and hence let itself go! You'd then have a long haired green hippy on your hands – and remember long hair only looks good on a woman and an Afghan Hound ... oh and a mop!

Trees with Degrees Draw Prehistoric Cheese!

Have you ever watched a dog having a shit? Eh? I mean have you ever really, really watched he/she/it doing its business? No? Well before I go into that, and I know you can't wait for me to explore this 'doggy-doo' theme (and are as excited as me at the prospect) … I'm thinking what is actually the correct salutation for addressing one of our canine friends?

Oh and before we explore that theme (that's two themes on the go at once … arghh), who the fuck thought it was appropriate to call dogs canine? Eh? I mean they're not made of freaking tin and look nothing like a metallic vessel for storing foodstuffs in (that's the can bit if I've lost you already) … and are not all aged 9! Nope! They're lovable creatures and all cuddly and woolly – okay furry (unless of course if they're wearing a jumper – but hey, only in winter … or after a really bad haircut) and they come (steady you rude person) in all blooming ages, from 0 to … well loads of years. Anyway – 'canine' my arse … it's all bollox … it's a dog. Yup, a dog is just that … a plain old straightforward dog! Unless of course it's a horse … hang on though … that's a bit too surreal even for moi. Since you've mentioned surreal (did you … or was it me) – here's a

207

thought for you. Question: How many Salvador Dali's does it take to change a lightbulb? Answer: A fish!

Yup – I'm really wired to the moon now … err okay, make that every day!

So where was I … oh yeah doggy salutation … no not saturation, as that's when they piss they're pants (if not going 'commando' … err which they usually do thinking about it) – after drinking too much water or even beer – but only if it's a 'Sibeerian Husky' (see what I did there … no … err okay). Hey, there's a thought – we always say a dog pants – but that's the one thing they hardly ever wear … yup pants. Well that and bras and waistcoats and cravats … oh and lots of other items of attire (it's not its clothing) I suppose! Imagine though if they did wear clothes? Wow! Would men dogs just wear one pair of trousers or two pairs … or one pair but with 4 legs? Hey, and would that still be classified as a 'pair' or a 'quad' … a quad of trousers? And what about girl doggies – how would a brassier (love that word … but don't know why) work. How many cups would that garment require – 4, 6, 8 … I never counted how many boobies girl doggies have … no really, I haven't … but I'll wager it's more than 2.

Anyway – you've got me digressing again, so doggy salutation. Is it a he, she or it? Now if a boy dog is a 'dog' and a girl dog is a 'bitch' who the heck's the 'it'? Is the 'it' a cross dressing transsexual dog – pre or post transgender operation? Or is it just a fog (typo – meant 'dog') who just wants to express its non-conformist freedom and expand the stereotypical <<big word, word – Alert>> sexual barriers? And what about calling a boy dog a 'dog'? I mean come on really … what a complete lack of imagination there by our ancestors – thick as pig-shit (or dog-shit for that matter) or what! No wonder our ancestors all lived in caves without cable TV or coffee percolators <<a silly word for a coffee machine, word – Alert>>. I mean how thick were those animal-skin clad big-foreheaded dudes? It's a freaking good job though they didn't use dog skins to keep out the elements or there wouldn't have been any doggies in the world today. And then this e-mail would've had never been written or would've been all about cats – which of course it's not. Oh and calling a girl dog a 'bitch'. How rude is that … most girl dogs I've known have been perfect ladies … although I've also known a few ladies who've been perfect dogs! Oh, and how unfair is it in regards to their male offspring? Those poor fuckers are simply 'sons of bitches'. Oh, oh … and their daughters are even worse – bitches of bitches! Bloody charming that is and what's the world coming to?

So – quickly, and unfortunately perhaps, back to dogs having a shit! Have you ever seen the face on a dog when it's having a shit? Eh … all smug and proud, and like – 'hey look at me … I'm having a shit!' They really think they're the dog's bollocks – and really proud of their activity – like a dog with two dicks … and that's probably something to be very proud of.

Their little head moves slowly from side to side as they look around like an absent-minded meerkat, looking vainly for his slippers after he'd forgotten where he put them! God knows what shitting dogs are looking for – certainly not toilet paper. Oh no, they've got their lovely tongues for that – and love nothing better than to come and lick their human buddies faces straight after they've had a nice relaxing dump! I shit you not … er, but they do. Oh, and don't let them lick inside your fucking mouth either (as they just always wanna do), especially after they come scampering excitedly from behind a

209

hedge or out of a bush. You can bet your bottom (rather apt) dollar that they've just been for a 'relaxing of their sphincter' (google that, mutha-fuckas) and opening of their 'bomb-doors' ... and have just finished really ruining the day of some poor beetles and ants with a shit storm from hell.

Thinking about it though, as both you and I are now, dogs are really so very lucky in so much as they are able to actually lick their own behinds. I mean how amazing would that be if we humans could each lick our own bottoms? How cool and awesome would that be eh ... and think how much money you'd save in bog-roll (bum-wad, toilet paper) each year. Stacks of cash that you could spend on other random and more important stuff – like ... err Columbian fresh ground coffee, lava lamps or nail varnish!

But hey ... alas we can't lick our own bum-holes though ... believe me I've tried enough times! Ermm ... maybe I shouldn't have mentioned that as you're probably thinking now that I'm a bit of a weirdo right now if you hadn't already arrived at that quite obvious conclusion.

Anyhow, they also, when having a 'Donald Trump', wear a kinda 'side-smile' that only dogs have ... you know like that 'Col. Hannibal Hayes' (google him) geezer outta the A-Team (google them maybe) with a cigar hanging out the side of his chops. Actually I'm thinking that a 'sides lips raised smile' is actually quite a cool look – I've just tried it in the bathroom mirror – don't worry though – I wasn't doing my business at the time. Now I'm not advocating <<educated word, word – Alert>> you going out and buying a cigar and placing it carefully so it's protruding <<fuck me, another educated word, word – Alert>> out of the side of your gob – as smoking is bad for you – even if it does cure fish. But you might wanna walk about with that cool doggy – 'I'm just having a shit dude' side-smile on your face as it might increase your street 'cred'. Or get you a stay at the 'funny farm' … with a 'straight-jacket' as a fashion accessory. I'm not actually sure which.

And as well as looking cool – dogs also wear a very concentrated look on their faces whilst having a plop. God knows why – I mean it's not exactly rocket science is it! Now everybody has to go for a number two – well except for the Queen of England (who has a butler do it for her) and very rich and famous individuals (who have their 'people' do tasks like this for them). You've also probably had one or more (hopefully more otherwise you be so full of shit by now) poops in your life and as such you'll know it's a pretty easy and straightforward procedure. There is no need whatsoever to concentrate. Mind you, and in a doggie's defence, I always prefer to 'go alone' and therefore have never actually seen the look on my face … and whether I'm wearing a concentrated expression … or indeed a side-smile? I think the next time I've got the need to go and sit on the 'chod-bin' (toilet) I'll bring a little hand held vanity mirror and watch myself … and as I'm on a prune and baked beans diet … I'll be going soon!

Oh and finally, as it's time for my medicine, and rather appropriately on this theme … I was out walking my dog earlier when an old granny shouted, "You make sure you pick that shit up."

I said, "Calm down, luv, let me wipe my fucking ass first!"

Oversized Bats in Plasticine Hats?

Now then, now then, now then … have you ever had one of those days when you go to the bog (the toilet BTW, and not some sopping wet muddy field) four times and on at least three of them you've ended up making a complete fucking mess all over the seat (if you haven't lifted it up), the bowl rim (if you have lifted it up) and the floor regardless of how you've addressed the previous two lifting actions? Oh and don't forget your soggy feet!

Well I have. Oh and in case you're wondering if I'm talking about a number one mess, or that made by you having the number two variety … I'm pleased to advise that I'm referring to that made by me emptying my bladder as opposed to my bowels … although I have before unfortunately performed both acts of downstairs offloadery <<new word that rolls smoothly off the tongue, word -Alert>> consecutively at the same time (have I just repeated myself there?). Anyway … total bathroom carnage.

Yup this act of mess makery <<hey … another just-now-made-up word that looks the part, word – Alert>> comes as a random and not every day, by any means, consequence of you having a slash. Now of course when I say 'you' I mean 'you' as in 'male', 'man', 'bloke', 'fella' … (fuck me standing up I'm glad there ain't a tax on punctuation marks!) and not 'you' as in a 'lady'. You see if you're of the female type then this sort of thing doesn't happen to you as you sit so eloquently on the aforementioned bog – like the Queen of England. And do so whether you're having a pee or a poo … as you're offloadery (this'll be in the Oxford English Dictionary soon with a few more mentions … just you see) machinery is far better designed than that of us blokes' bits. Well that is of course until you're out on the lash and get caught short, as we men can simply, but quite covertly, fumble our one-eyed-trouser-snakes out of our pants, lean against a wall/hedge and let loose … emptying the contents of our bladder.

Christ (he's not actually involved mind) … we don't even have to hold the fucker (apt as its other function), as the sides of your fly's and the steadying effect of your elasticated undies providing a perfect 'pee-platform' making it a pretty easy to just (and as the '80s painted face punk-popster would warble) stand and deliver! Heck – I can even walk and pee … and can do so hands free! Never tried this? Well blooming well do. But hey only if you're a bloke, as shuffling along down the street or beach with your panties round your ankles whilst looking like a pregnant duck with rickets … ain't a good look.

Now whilst we guys can perform all these 'ease of pees' (like what I did there) activity whilst out and about, it's a different story altogether when we feel the urge to go and exercise a bit of bladder release in the very comfort of our own homes. Oh yeah … a different fucking story altogether … but one that as mentioned earlier, happens infrequently and quite unexpectedly. But it should be so simple all the time though – shouldn't it. I mean it's the same friggin action as when you're outside and need to 'splash the slash'. And better still … you take even more care when you 'point Percy at the porcelain' indoors as this is your house and your bathroom … and not a neighbour's garden wall or the doorway of a charity shop. It should just be a straightforward case of hold the python (well in my case and not a worm – honest) point, squeeze, then slowly release the gripped pressure and pee! Bullseye, target hit and frankly easy-squeezey-lemon-peesy' … it does indeed taste like lemon juice – but how I actually know that is for another time.

But oh no, and no matter how accurate you are (and believe me … I can usually piss through the eye of dwarf's sewing needle), instead of hitting the pan … it goes all crazy and sprays frigging everywhere … like there's an elephants foot holding your knob (there isn't BTW as I'm not into that sorta thing). You know … like when you accidentally let go of a hose pipe … and soak everything within 'soak everything reaching distance!' Yup when one of these 'can piss-can't-piss' days occur it's a real friggin annoyance as it turns what normally is a 39 (typed '30' there as '39s' a tad too precise) second act into one that lasts a couple of blooming minutes as you get down on hands and knees to wipe up the spillage off the seat, rim, floor and wall(s) with bits of toilet paper – which was never really designed for the job.

And so the culprit for all this cockery (I'm at it again with the new words) carnage? Well it's not as 'you' women (if you're not a guy reading this or if you're a post-op tranny) would believe … laziness or clumsiness. It's not even got anything to with a bloke being under the influence of alcohol – as it can happen on a day when you're as sober as a judge … err a priest … err, well let's just say before you've had a sniff of the happy sauce. Nope, the culprit is God. Now I don't actually mean that the big white bearded fella up in the sky likes to have a random 'Turkish' at our expense and as such makes our dicks not work properly or moves the toilet an inch or two to the right or left at the very second we unloose the juice. No, the culprit's 'foreskin' … yup that skin that's at the forefront (hence its name – maybe … I ain't checked a biology book) of us bloke's cocks. And of course as God created us blokes in his image … it's him that gave this stupid extra knob-skin flappy thing to us and as such it's his flipping fault!

Now what is flipping heck is this foreskin foreskin for? Oh and sod off 'Delete Repeated Word' notification – it's meant to be repeated? I mean it's not like my knob's gonna get cold and need a sorta skin crafted cravat to keep out the elements in winter time is it? Nope … its kept nice and snuggly in my y-fronts … which are always 2 sizes too small … so the sweat in there alone keeps my pecker all nice and snuggly like a blooming sauna … even right at the Bishop's hat end. So what is the foreskin actually for? I mean it's just a wrinkly scarf isn't it (couldn't really use cravat twice in one paragraph), that's self-remote controllably retractable … all it takes is a quick rush of blood (which I can easily get from a quick glance at a 'wank-mag' or a fleeting glimpse in the mirror) and off it goes. My big fella starts to solidify and just like the retractable roof on Wimbledon Centre Court on a sunny day after a rainy night … my foreskin disappears like a magician's assistant … although there's no puff of smoke. Hey presto it's there one minute … next and its gone.

Yup … the reality of the situation is that the fire skin (tried to type 'foreskin' there and ouch … the other would be a tad painful) is just a waste of skin and so gets in the way when we guys have a tinkle. Now normally as

I've mentioned – this isn't a problem … as it kinda automatically retracts just enough to allow our 'jap's-eye' to syphon said python. But of course occasionally, and on this very random day each month when you couldn't piss properly even if you're life depended on it … your extra skin just seems to close up so awkwardly and the result is like a when you put your fingers across the end of that gushing hose pipe I mentioned earlier. And so, your perfectly innocent attempt to complete a normal bodily function – just side-sprays out everywhere – except into the freaking bog where's it's supposed to friggin go! Arghh. Hey perhaps this is a man's 'time of the month' and therefore maybe we don't get off as lightly as you ladies think. I mean, okay … so you womenfolk have to 'endure' a little bleeding leakage every month – but at least yours stops when you get all middle aged and frumpy. No such luck for us poor blokes … we have to endure this monthly inconvenience and sometimes foot soaking for ever … and if anything, it gets worse as we get older – as we've gotta add our failing eyesight and shaking hands into the friggin equation as well!

And so … and on one randy (typed 'random' there – but it's even harder to control the directional flow of a pee when the old-man's standing to attention) day every month or so you'll slash, splash make a fucking hash (of it). And this won't happen just the once, oh no … it'll afflict you throughout that particular 'piss-poor' day and every time take a leak … when you take a leak – by fuck you'll frigging leak all over the show.

Hey … but maybe the fact of the matter is that it's in reality just me, and I've just simply got a wonky foreskin clad dick and hence this pissing all over the porcelain, tiles, walls, feet is just unique to me? Hmm … I hope not

... although perhaps the lack of waterproof male pissing devices in chemists could be a clue that it is in fact just me? Oh, and ... the most recent occurrence wax (typed 'was' there – but hey, I actually need my bikini line done) whilst I was on an all-inclusive holiday in Spain. Now in my defence the clue is in the words 'all-inclusive' and as such I've gotta admit that was absolutely puddled most of the week ... and as such my bladder was no doubt stretched to beyond friggin bursting point most days. In fact, no ... every day!

And so ... Spain and my all-inclusive holiday of alcohol debauchery <<a great word that has nothing to do with a girl who likes firing a bow and arrow, word – Alert>> Well ... oh ... now before I go on and ramble on about Spain a bit ... can I very speedily please if you don't mind (I'm gonna anyhow as in reality I don't really need your permission as I'm in the writing-driving seat here and you're ... err ... not even here, you're ... err ... there) go back to the very opening words in this latest pile of poodle poo ... which were of course a kind of 'stutter'.

And so a 'stutter'. Now why the fuck isn't it 'sstutter' ... eh? I mean, c'mon ... it's a very poor excuse for a self-descriptive word (which surely they all really should be) and as such is another example of one of those words that don't sound or look like they mean. You know ... like really 'transparent' which actually (and maybe unbelievably ... or maybe not) isn't your dad in a skirt and a wig or your mum smoking a pipe whilst wearing Y-fronts. But then I suppose to be fair to 'transparent', it's is just a misunderstood and ambiguous word with potential dual meanings, and what I really wanna explore is words that have or don't have the required descriptive 'umph'. Or in other words 'onomatopoeia', or words that deliver in their literally meaning exactly what they sound like they say they do.

So, 'onomatopoeia' words, or to put it scientifically (it's not BTW) – ones that phonetically imitate the source of the sound they describe (do fucking what)? Now although it sounds like that complete shite Latin nonsense again … it's actually not … it's Greek. Now you may never have realized this before (or cared enough to even think about), but Greek and Latin are virtually the same languages. Oh yeah, although to be fair to Latin (just this freaking once though I swear) Greek is written in a crazy bonkers alphabet which in truth makes it even shittier than that 'Roman' speak. In all honesty though – they're both all Greek to me. Anyhow, I digress and must always try to quell my Latinitus (a phobia and dislike shitty languages … maybe), so let's very, very, very (triple repeat to convince you this'll be brief) quickly look at a few examples of the crazy word that is 'onomatopoeia'.

Well there's (this'll pan this rant out even further) …

* Splash
* Growl
* Flutter
* Bang
* Thud
* Belch
* Gurgle
* Guffaw
* Whisper
* Whoosh

* Yikes

* Splatter

* Bonk

* Meow

So there you have it. And as you now follow the flow or get the gist you can easily see that the boring old non-descriptive word 'stutter' should really be sssttttutterrr! Now I think we've been short changed here – mind you how on earth did I actually get here? Not on the Earth, mind you – as that was via a stork delivering me in a sling in his oversized drooling fish smelling gob ... but here – to this particular ridiculous 'wordy' topic?

Oh, and let's not forget the most crackers of all of these descriptive words – 'blowjob' (which links this bit back to the last but one bit) ... as its neither an occupation (well maybe for a 'one-trick-pony' prostitute) nor does it involve at any point the forced exhaling of air. Surely it's inhaling – so why not 'suck-job' or an 'SJ'? Eh? I mean that would be even more descriptive wouldn't it – and be still be 'onomatopoeia' ... and fun ... err, maybe – but not for me. Oh no, as although I'm a man – and as such should be qualified to one fly (well that's involved but actually typed 'openly' there) talk about fellatio, or cock feeding, or orally syphoning the python ... I'm actually not. Alas no – as the sad truth is that I've only ever experienced just the one Blowjob. And I didn't like it one bit! In fact, I really hated it. I mean it took me ages to get the taste outta my mouth ... err?

And so, and talking of my recent vacation in Spain again (remember that time in your life before I got that complete and utter 'onomatopoeia' nonsense into your flipping head), have you ever observed Brits abroad?

219

Well fuck me backwards (actually don't please as my rusty sheriff's badge is only used handling medium sized objects … jettisoning only BTW … honest), but as you now know (yawn) – I've just recently (or a long time ago dependent on when you're reading this) returned from vacation to Majorca and witnessed the complete tomfoolery <<ridiculous but lovely old English word for silliness, word – Alert>> of these half-brained morons whilst on they're on their summer jollies.

Actually, and you're probably gonna hate me for this (if you don't already), but I'm gonna stop this nonsense here before I fear you fall into a deeper state of unconsciousness than Sleeping Beauty on Valium … or die of boredom. Or perhaps no – and you've been wishing the shite would end half way through the very first paragraph – and as such are now grinning the biggest sigh of relief since that bearded vampire bloke who lived in a stable with his perfect mum and wood-working loving dad many, many years ago, not only realized he was impervious to metal spikes but also freaking immortal as well. You know … that Jesus bloke with the long beard and even longer hair – inherited from his 'real biological old dad' who as well as ruling the universe – also had a fear of barbers. Oh and before you put pen to paper or finger to keyboard or metal clip to pigeon's foot to write me a complaint about my apparent and unnecessary heresy (had to Google how to spell that) in comparing God's son to a bloodsucking bat … please calm down … I'm not. I mean in no way am I saying that Jesus wore a black cloak (with a red velvet lining – they always do in the movies don't they …), disliked his own reflection, sunbathing and ridiculous French (had to be) breath stinking herbs. Oh no. But he did hate crosses … didn't he? He must've. Err … let's move very quickly on please and if your very religious just pretend that last bit was a dream … and now your awake, back in the room and as such it never happened.

So anyway … I'll revisit Spain and bonkers Brits abroad in a future or precious ('previous' even … although it may well be of incredible value to you when you read it/have read it … maybe?) rant and as such release you now from any more undue and continued suffering. Oh (oh … shit), but before I do truly put a final nail in the coffin of this cacophony (not really as that particular Latin pooh means sounds – and not words … but hey, I was just trying to look clever) of words, I'm just gonna make one very final U-turn. Now not the sheep type mind, as that'd be a 'ewe-turn' … which would be … err … crazy, but one that takes you back to my recent mention of my birth and the stork. Oh and please don't be alarmed if this pants rant just ends suddenly and soon after this next diversion as although I'm clearly on literary 'fire' here … even I've got my limits. After all … I'm only human … although only just!

Now when I say 'stork', I am of course referring to the winged bird (don't they all have … well unless they're female humans – who only have 'bingo-wings') variety and not of course the ridiculously named British brand of margarine. I mean to say (no, I'm actually just saying so why I mentioned the words 'mean to' there is beyond even me), let's face it … a fucking bird delivering a friggin baby is bonkers enough … never mind an oversized yellow and blue painted plastic tub of tasteless fake butter performing midwifery (great word) duties! And anyhow it would have to be the feathered no-arms but instead winged variety of stork … as the foul tasting margarine ones have no eyes to see where they're delivering said baby, no wings to actually get

221

them to said baby's address and worse still (or just equally as worse) … no friggin mouth, sorry 'beak' to hold said baby in! And anyhow … I don't even know who in deepest biblical history (gotta be as Jesus was the first ever baby wasn't he) was even responsible for dispatching the freaking silly big mouthed white birds with baby in mouth – let alone those awkward environmental-unfriendly tubs stuffed with slimy wannabe … but could never be … butter. But mind you – maybe I'm taking even more bollox than a normal bollox-per-rant-tax would allow because I've just remembered that that (allowable stutter alert) 'Stork' margarine was actually fully entitled 'Stork SB', so maybe these tubs of lard actually were/still are responsible for delivering babies as the 'SB' actually stands for 'sending babies'! Hmmm …?

Or maybe not … as even for crazy me, and one of my usual run-of-the-mill bonkers rants, I'm probably in grave danger of truly stretching the realms of both credibility and reality here. And anyhow … if we really were delivered at birth by a somehow able to fly, see and carry – carton of solidified cow's piss – aka margarine … then why weren't we all covered in greasy slime when we were born … eh? Oh hang about though …

Quaggers!

Spontaneous Sweets Seek
Serendipitous Streets?

Ever wondered why two odd numbers always add up to an even number and yet two even numbers never ever add up to an odd one?

No, well tough luck as I do ... and even worse ... maybe they do!

Now you might think at this precise moment in time (although not at the very same moment in time mind you, as I'm typing this now and you're reading this at a later date) that there's no way (or 'know weigh' if you're either a) illiterate and fluent in 'Pidgin English', or b) a psychic who can foretell how heavy people are ... err?) that two even numbers can ever add up to an odd one. Well no, and the totally stupendous news for you (and better than you discovering that you can piss pink champagne) is that I'm gonna thrust open the 'stuff is what stuff is and that's that' curtains that are drawn across your mind and let the 'ooh, that could actually be reality' light shine in. But before I do that (and you know what's coming next) ... I'm gonna just revert back to the seemingly bizarre attempt or need to explain the mention of the 'precise moment in time' reference just before there ... which is no doubt gonna make you groan louder and with more angst and energy than a heavily dilated pregnant cow with a vet's hand wedged up its ass!

And so, when I, albeit very briefly, started to waffle back there in paragraph 1 (and I do, oh so very easily) about the factuality <<typed that last word and wasn't really sure it was gonna give me an underlined-red-dot-no-such-word, word – Alert>> of the use of the phrase 'precise moment in time' and its implausibility and feasibility of being a reality (wow a lot 'itys' there), I wasn't mucking around. I mean, I might've written this bollox months (or even years if it's now been consigned to where it could actually belong – the vaults of a rural library in Azerbaijan) before you've had the great fortune to be able to bask and marvel in its literary gems. And if so then you'd either need a spy webcam built into my iPad Mini to observe my rancid ramblings real time, or a DeLorean with a flux capacitor fitted (as standard 'cos I'll bet they cost a bit), to be able to consider stuff at the – 'this precise moment' that this was actually being scribbled by me. Now whilst I'm not sure whether or not you actually own an '80s 'Gull-Winged' DMC sports car – I'm pretty sure you haven't infiltrated my iPad thingy with a webcam thingy. Hang on though and 'fuck me standing up' – there just one God dang minute (or a standard minute if it's shorter) – as I've just accidentally touched a random button on my iPad and all of a sudden there was this middle-aged bald weirdo staring at me looking like a right twat and who not only seemed to be able to mimic every facial expression I was making – but was in my fucking lounge – sitting right where I was! WTF? I'll tell you what – there's some blooming clever hackers about these days … and ugly hairless ones … eh?

Oh and when I mentioned DMC back there, I was of course referring to the acronym (not sure what the acronym for acronym is though) for the DeLorean Motor Corporation, who of course made the time-traveling car for the 'Back to the Future' movie trilogy, and not that '80s (I think) and one hit wonder (I'm sure) totally wank band 'Run DMC'. And whilst on this theme (we are now), why didn't thermometers (typed 'the makers' back there … but even my iPad Mini keys are too small for my average sized … or maybe not, fingers) of the BTTF (another acronym) franchise make a fourth or even a fifth movie? Were they actually 'in the know' and as such simply realized that a fourth movie would be an even number and therefore would (no could) never add up odd number, even (apt) if they then made another two, four or even (apt again) six? And if so (and it's a real whopper of a gigantic 'if') why the frigging hell would they even (getting silly now) actually care about odds making evens, but not vice-versa … as surely this is only a ridiculous notion in my half-witted head? Or did they actually own a real working fluxed-up DMC (no, and again not the 'self-abusing' band) and saw that as the piss-poor 3rd instalment would be received as such complete and utter shite … that any subsequent ones would've disappeared off the cinema going radar faster than hot shit off a heated shovel? And therefore they simply thought to themselves – 'hey guys – lets ditch this farcical nonsense and fooking scraper … quicker than, err … hot shit off a hot shovel!'

And so back to the odd thing about even numbers that's actually, if you think about it, not really that odd at all. I mean I've been thinking about this age-old problem for … well … at least the last 4 minutes and I think I've actually cracked it! Well okay, I'll level with you, as I'm really an honest bloke even if I do spout a lot of ambiguous, implausible and hard to believe irrelevant shite. The truth is that I've prolly (short for 'probably' but importantly rhymes with jolly, which I always am … eh?) thought about this for maybe 5 mins … well I will have now by the end of this sentence. Yup … 5 mins … on and 10 seconds right, right … (wait for it) … now!

Oh and please forgive me, but I must really, just really – and very briefly (it will be honest-ish) refer back to the mention of the word 'rhymes'. Now whilst I'm no poet, and I know it (0h <oops 'o'> hang about though maybe I am), I'm just at this point quite randomly drawn to thinking about LeAnn Rimes … or Leanne Rhymes in proper English, which clearly here parents weren't fluent in at her birth … or in the following years as they never corrected their clumsy spelling mistake. Now who you ask? Well it's no less than that U.S. country and pop singer and wannabe actress of the very same name (although not the correct English one BTW and instead the silly pissed-up parents' version). Oh – and at this point may I just apologies for the aforementioned <<great long word simply meaning 'previous', word – Alert>> mention of '-ish', as I'm starting to ramble on a bit now about this 'rhymes' bit. But fear thee not – I'm not going to devote a whole rant to this nonsense. Oh no … to that degree I won't go (ooh rhyming par-excellence).

And so … what a crazy girl's name that poor old songstress ended up with as a clear result of her parents either smoking dope at the time of her christening … or just simply being – dopes.

I mean 'Leanne Rhymes' … WTF? How totally bonkers is that as a) with what (it don't tell you that does it), and b) … and the no doubt reason for a) … is that the fact of the matter is, is that Leanne doesn't actually

Rome (typed 'rhyme' there but anyhow ...) with anything else. Well not in English anyhow ... and as I've already mentioned on a good few occasions in the past (or future if this is your 1st Pantsrantasy <<new word for the near orgasmic experience that overwhelms you when you read a pants rant, word – Alert>>), that's the only language that counts, as other countries' pathetic rambling 'jibber jabber' aren't worth a wank in a sweet-shop! 'Ooh how unfair' I hear you groan (especially if you are indeed having a 'wank' and even more so, in a candy store), but it's not – as English is really the only credible language out there isn't it? Oh ... and remember before you chastise me for being pro-English ... I'm not ... I'm an inbred Viking. Yup I hail (apt) from a tiny, cold little windswept rock where the sun only shines on TV – as the Norwegian mega pop band (no really) once warbled, and even more apt as they were Vikings as well.

And so very quickly back to Leanne. I mean it's complete an utter bollox as it's one of the few words out there that rhymes with fuck bloody all ... and it doesn't even rhyme with that ('fuck', 'bloody' or 'all'). Nope, there is in fact no such like-rhyming word in the universe that's a match for the ridiculous 'Leanne' and if you can find one I'll send your free copy of the world's best ever poetry book ... 'LeAnn Rimes Greatest Rhymes'! Oh, and as I'm feeling generous (don't worry 'Gen' likes a good manhandling) I'll even send you a copy if you can simply think of just one other word in the English language that doesn't have a rhyming partner ... you know – like 'orange', 'bulb' or 'angel' ... oh bollox ... what's your address for me to send the book?

And so finely, err 'finally' I'd better get back to me cracking the numbers code thingamajig that's has baffled intellects for centuries (maybe) and me for minutes (definitely). Well I'm delighted to advise that's its quite simple really, and actually as clear as day. Well okay, maybe a very overcast or foggy day as in fact actually it's not really that clear at all ... as my solution is called 'invisible numbers'. Now before you reach for the 'off' button of your iPhone or Android device, or tablet ... or just reach for the tablets, please let me attempt to explain myself (well – qualify my numeric solution and not an in-depth rationale about me) by means of a mathematical example.

Oh, and very, very quickly may I once again go back to the aforementioned and ridiculously entitled 'Android device'. Now whilst I've got absolutely no problems with the word 'device' – the terminology 'Android' (see – I can't even type it) is just so incredibly fucked up. I mean who the frig was this Ann lady who gave her name to second rate phones and stuff, and when or why (or both) did she decide it was clever to drop an 'n' or even (still apt ... and we'll get to it – honest) an 'ne' ... if she had the posher version of the name?

Indeed, Android is just a charlatan masquerading <<two great words in near succession, words – Alert>> as a realistic alternative to the iPhone/iPad which in reality ... it's quiet clearly not. Nope – God gave Adam his first phone thousands of years ago – and if an Apple was good enough for that ... then it's good enough for you and me. Do you know what ... a thought has just crept into my microscopic brain and as such I'm now going to dedicated a whole (or in part as I'll no doubt go off on one) to mobile phones. Now I know you'll be feverishly excited at the prospect of this – but please be patient.

And so very, very, very finally, and truly this time – here's my proof that two even numbers actually do add up to an odd one. And you're gonna be impressed as I've got a formulaic example for you stick in your pipe and smoke … but hey, only if you smoke as I'm not inciting you to start:

EXAMPLE 1 (there's only one BTW):

$2 + 2 = X$?

Or

$1(2)$ and $2\ (2) = X$?

So

$1 + 2 + 2 + 2 = 7$

Therefore

$2 + 2 = 7$.

Fact … and 'even' or 'oddly' it adds up to an odd number! Eureka!

Now accepted … there's a couple of 'unusual' missing (invisible) numbers that I've included in what would normally be a more common-place mathematical equation … but who's to say that I'm incorrect. I mean where is it written in the big book (the Bible) that $1 + 1 = 2$ or $6 - 1 = 5$ or even $4 + 4 = 8$ as opposed to 11 (as I've just demonstrated)? It's not – so I might actually be on to something here … it's gotta happen one day after all.

So okay – this formulaic miracle solution (no really) is indeed totally powered by the concept of the existence of 'invisible' numbers. "That's total rubbish," I hear you sneer … but why? I mean if maths has 'divisible' numbers … then why not 'invisible' ones … as they must be from the same numeric family as they're basically spelt the same. See ... I'll bet you're not feeling so smug now are you ... eh, eh (repeated for that 'I told you so effect').

Now maybe the reality of the situation is, is that those supposedly super-clever and academic (I'll come back to that – and that's a fact) Greek geezers who invented numbers and maths were either a) having a Turkish (which would've kinda ironic I guess), or b) got it so completely and totally fucking wrong! So okay ... they might have had nicely manicured intellectual beards and been able to carry off (well nearly) the wearing of girly togas (skirts for ancient transvestites – like those Roman wankers) ... but were they a tailor (I typed 'actually' there ... and boy, they certainly needed one) any good at flipping sums?

Okay, so I know that Greece had an apparent soup-thick (not consume though) gene-pool of intellectual talent, what with it being able to boast Pythagoras, Plato, Archimedes, Socrates, Aristotle and the crazily named Hippocrates (named after a method of transporting huge grey-skinned mammals), but we're they actually really any good at maths ... or 'math' as those crazy letter-dropping-slang-loving Yanks would say? I mean okay ... maybe they were 'clever dicks' (not penises with brains though ... as, as every lady knows dicks don't have 'em), but perhaps the truth is that sums were unbelievably, but actually in reality, 'all Greek' ... to them! Now as crackers as this might sound, as this bunch of bearded intellects collectively discovered very important stuff like how to measure the width of pies, how to correctly to fill a bath tub with water so it doesn't flood the floor ... and even democracy, I might actually be on to something here as how come they never thought of 'invisible' numbers ... eh? Answer me that then. You can't!

Or maybe they actually did discover this numerical odd/even fact before moi (or 'me' in proper 'non-Froggish-speak'), but were just so very wrapped up in their calculations, and so totally confused and frustrated by having to jot down every bit of calculus on a stone tablet (not an Apple one) with a chisel in their ridiculously crazy illegible language, that they just simply missed the obvious. You know, like – they couldn't see the wood for the trees ... with the trees being their stupid back-to-front-upside-down-inside-out freaking letters – which even make Russian look sane. Or maybe not.

Mind your things haven't changed much over the last couple of thousand years have they? I mean look how they've royally fucked up with their numbers lately. And alas things have just got worse for those crazy Ouzo swigging, plate smashing, wooden horse loving Mediterranean fools, as I've just heard that Greece has reduced its exports of hummus and taramasalata ... as they fearful of a double-dip recession!

Anyhow ... I better stop ranting now as I've just felt a very odd and quite spontaneous urge to commence the motion which leads to a dispatch-hatch commotion. You know ... the once, maybe twice (or even more if you've got a 'jelly-botty') daily activity of opening one's Sphinx (I actually typed 'sphincter' there, but hey ... it kinda works) and partaking <<a silly, but at the same time clever word with the same meaning if split in half and the back half placed at the front – with an extra 't' added for good measure, word – Alert>> in the activity of 'seeing a few friends off to the coast'! In other words – I need a number two ... which in reality isn't odd at all as it's even. Well unless that is I do two of them consecutively (that's one after the other to normal and 'non-intellectual' or posh people like you and me), as then by my calculations that would be odd ... remember?

Ohhhh shit (literally) ... I really, really should have stopped typing at the start of that that last paragraph ...

Quaggers!

AND FINALLY'S:

You'll be glad.

Quick question … who the fuck picks up a guide dog's shit?

I don't wish to boast, but I finished my 14-day diet in just 4 hours and 17 minutes!

Life is like a cock. Sometimes it gets hard for no reason!

Shin bone … a device used for finding furniture in the dark!

I'm trying to give up sexual innuendos … but it's hard … so very hard!

So Christmas … what was it called before that Jesus bloke gave his surname to it?

Castration … it takes balls!

That band 'Snow Patrol'. I love them … but what do they do in the summer?

In Iran everyone's scared of spiders, but in Iraq, no phobia?

I use my Ouija board while I'm in a bath full of yoghurt. I like to dabble in the Yakult!

I used to have a job drilling holes for water. It was well boring!

Someone hit me with a sweet smelling burning stick. I was incensed!

I got into a pointless argument with the manager at the local garden centre when he suggested I needed decking!

Red roses – check!

Barry White album – check!

Scented candles – check!

Tonight, that little hot minx of a wank sock won't know what's hit it.

I used to go out with a prostitute. Now I'm not saying she was ugly … but her pimp drove a Skoda!

I bought a new pair of shoes today but when I got them home I realized that one was a slip on and the other one had laces? I blame myself … on the box it said … Taiwan!

What do you call a psychic midget that escaped from prison?

'A small, medium, at large.'

Me and my buddies at the gun club often go to the French cheese shop … just to shoot the Bries.

Proof that being kicked in the balls is more painful than childbirth. Several months after being kicked in the balls a male does not say, "I think I want another kick in the balls."

My kitten is very cute but he does get everywhere. Recently, he got his feet caught under my Sky TV box, and now my TV's permanently on paws.

I tried to buy my missus some eel skin trousers for her birthday, but they're almost impossible to get hold of!

Guess what my biggest kitchen utensil is? It's ma sieve.

My credit card company sent me a camouflaged bull. It's the hidden charges you have to watch out for.

My doctor told me that I have to stop drinking French liqueurs as they're causing my internal organs to fill up with melted cheese – apparently absinth makes the heart grow fondue.

I read a book about World War II that was only four pages long – it was Abridged Too Far.

I really can't stand people who think they're worse off than everybody else. Take my mate Dave … he's brilliant. He had a bad accident where he lost his voice and both his legs … Does he make a song and dance about it? Does he frig!

I bought one of those 'Impressionist' paintings recently, but my cat scratched it. Now it's a 'clawed Monet'.

I've been in hospital … but just to let you all know that I'm back home now. The doctors think that I might have that 'Pneumotramicroscopicsilicovolcanokoniosis' … but at the moment it's hard to say.

Never ever leave sulphuric acid in a metal beaker ...
that's an oxidant waiting to happen!

As me old dad used to say ... "Son take those off,
they're your sisters!"

Those smoking patches are absolutely fucking
rubbish ... there a bugger to roll and they won't stay lit!

Calories: are the little bastards that get together at
night in your closet and sew your clothes tighter. My
closet is infested with the little fucking shits.

My girlfriend smiled at me as she held my cock in
her hand and said ... "Hey love, what's the difference
between pink and purple?"

"I don't know honey," I said.

She sneered and said ... "The fucking grip!"

Those speed bumps in the road are rubbish ... if
anything they slow you down!

As my old dad used to say ... "Son, put that back in
your pants ... you'll have someone's eye out!"

Oh look, it's snowing outside!

I'll update my Facebook status for all my friends ...

That don't have a fucking window of their own!

The main disadvantage of being an atheist is that there's nobody to talk to during an orgasm!

Now I'm not saying my first ever girlfriend wasn't very pretty – but if I'd had a dog as ugly as her ... I'd have shaven its ass and taught it to walk backwards!

How come monkeys are all hairy, yet have pink asses with no hair on ... whilst I'm as bald as a coot and I've got a big hairy ass? Perhaps Charles Darwin could friggin well explain that!

Shag ... a funny word isn't it?

To a smoker, it's a type of tobacco.

To an American, it's a type of dance.

To an ornithologist, it's a bird ...

Alas to me ... it's a rare event!

When I was a kid, you could go into a corner shop with 10 pence and come out with 3 cans of coke, 6 chocolate bars, 4 bags of crisps and a couple of comic books.

Not nowadays. There's fooking CCTV everywhere!

And there's a thing – never buy a mermaid tights!

I suffered the most ultimate sexual rejection last night ... I was masturbating and my hand fell asleep.

Whoever coined the phrase 'Cleanliness is next to Godliness' was talking out of his arse! I looked them up in the dictionary last night. 'Godly' and 'Godsend' are next to 'Godliness', whilst 'Cleanliness' was 353 friggin pages away!

I've had to sell my vacuum cleaner ... it was just gathering dust!

I suffer from Chronic Insomnia. But hey – I look on the bright side ... I've only got 3 sleeps till Christmas!

I know this guy who is an agnostic-dyslexic ... he doesn't believe in 'Dog'!

Remember – a lot of 'man stuff' looks really good on a woman ... but stubble isn't one of them.

If I ever find the guy who messed up my limb transplants, I'm going to kill him with my bear hands.

I've just saw a romantic lover riding circles around his fiancé on a unicycle whilst juggling 3 bouquets of flowers ... I thought, 'What a cupid stunt!'

"That's a massive fucking drawback" … as the veterinary said when about to perform the circumcision on the Bull elephant.

I went for a job interview last week.

So I went in and sat down with the boss.

The boss asked me, "So Mr Quaggan" (I prefer Gaz or Stud Muffin … but hey it was an interview) "what do you think is your worst quality?"

I said, "I'm probably too honest."

The boss said, "That's not a bad thing, I think being honest is a really good quality."

I replied, "I don't give a flying fuck what you think you fucking twat!"

I didn't get the job!

I've already started writing a follow-up to this book. I've made excellent progress so far.

I've got the page numbers done!

The other day I blooming well cut myself shaving. Now it really hurts when I pee!

Are you suffering from 'Deja Moo' … the feeling that you've heard this bullshit before?

I'm gonna taking part in the World 'Twerking Off' Championships this weekend ... well I think they said it was gonna be 'twerking off'?

People who say they suffer from constipation ... are they full of shit?

And very finally-finally, and on the same theme as the rest of this nonsense ...

The missus just said to me, "Our marriage has come to an end."

I said, "Fuck off ... only good things come to an end ..."

THAT'S IT ...

THERE'S NO MORE HERE!

THE END

Well ... until next time, and like night follows day (or is it the other way round) there will be a next time and that'll be coming your way faster than hot shit off a shovel.

You have been warned.